In Passing
A Collection

Danny Lalonde

When people ask what genre I write, I don't have a clean answer. *Horror* is what I usually say, but horror the way people think of horror is not what I'm interested in. Traditional horror novels and movies with monsters, aliens, and dark basements and closets aren't real enough for me. My characters are normal people who are forced to confront the everyday tragedies that shape who we are. I feel compassion for most of my characters whether they survive or not. Aristotle wrote about the purpose of art as being a catharsis, something external which helps us purge our internal anxieties. I don't want you to like my characters. I don't want you to feel anything close to "we have a lot in common." I imagine you pausing, maybe screaming, and then rushing on in a better direction. That's who these characters and stories are to me: a purge.

Self-publishing was once called Vanity Press. The notion is that a writer thinks they are so good that they skip all the vetting and editing of traditional agents and publishers with a sense of their own greatness. There are many vanity writers with storage spaces full of unsold books. In my case, a number of these stories have been vetted and published, sometimes by print magazines, sometimes by online publishers. Some of the other stories are fresh to this collection. I'm interested in writing differently, writing different types of stories. For a long time, I was plagued by a sense of my own inadequacy and impotence. In the words of one of my characters, "*I feel it in my chest all of the time now, the coming of death, the rushing in my ears, the muffled way the world sounds to me, as though my head is tied inside a bag of water.*" (Tom, *In the Way*). In my real life, I've moved past any feeling like this. My life is full of light and joy. I hope to leave these characters behind. Before I stuff them all in the trunk, these horrors deserve a day in the light. They have something to learn and maybe something to teach.

Once upon a time, short stories were everywhere. Every home had a coffee table full of magazines which included some variety of prose. Someone suggested that, any more, only writers read short stories. At the bottom of each story, I've included any publication history and notes related to what inspired the story, or recorded things I was thinking before or after I finished writing. Hopefully, the back stories pique your curiosity. Thanks to Philip for this consideration. Despite some of the stories having been published before, I re-edited each for this collection. Sometimes, the edit is just a tweak, sometimes more drastic changes are presented.

Beside these stories, I've written other things. In fact, I have dozens of stories. Every writer has a trunk full of work in progress, work abandoned, and work that will never claw its way from the detritus. I've only included my favourite pieces herein. I have published pieces that didn't make it here. Many of the stories included are themed around water and the struggles that come from being too far out and too long treading. This sense of being "un-grounded" is perhaps the unifying element of the collection. I'll let the literary critics formulate any deeper analysis of the work.

As far as publishing is concerned, there's a big difference between creating and selling. I've never been good at sales. The anxiety of knowing my darlings are out there trying to impress a potential agent or publisher sends me into itchy fits and I can't write at all.

Special thanks to the many writers I've worked with, students in writing classes I've taught, the Little Workshop of Horror group in Ottawa who have encouraged me along, and many friends and family who have read various drafts and iterations of these stories. Thanks to my son, Philip, who gave me a kick in the pants a few years ago and got me thinking about doing this project. Thank you to my wife, Janette, who patiently read through the manuscript looking for errors and gaffs. I'm sure that in the editing, we've missed some mistakes.

If you read this far into the foreword, let me close with a warning: Read one at a time. Don't binge the whole thing. Give each story and character careful consideration. Mark the space between you and them with that yellow tape police use, or circle the difficult parts with white chalk and walk away. Stay far away from the disaster. I welcome any comments, reviews, suggestions to lalonded12@gmail.com.

About the images

When film cameras were popular, every trip to the print shop inevitably resulted in a picture or two of nothing – confusing images of blurs, legs, thumbs, dusty sky. In choosing artwork for these stories, I parsed through my digital prints to find the images that have been included. They are of nothing in particular, but are meant to give an impression of something. If they're blurry or badly framed, it is intentional. I'm not sure who took many of

the photos. Mostly me, but maybe also other family members. My friend JR took this orange picture. I cut my own head off for fun.

Brian wants to walk on water. There are many things he wants to do, but Brian thinks that if he starts with the water that everything else will follow easily. So, early one Saturday morning while Beth and the kids are still in the cabin asleep, Brian clambers down the rocky slope to the water and onto the dock that leads into Otter Lake.

Brian slips out of his sandals, and stretches a tentative foot down over the still surface. Something like a prayer runs the length of his concentration and sounds like, *JesusFatherMotherMaryJoseph* over and over again. He exercises great faith because the endeavour demands it. Most everything he wants to do requires great faith.

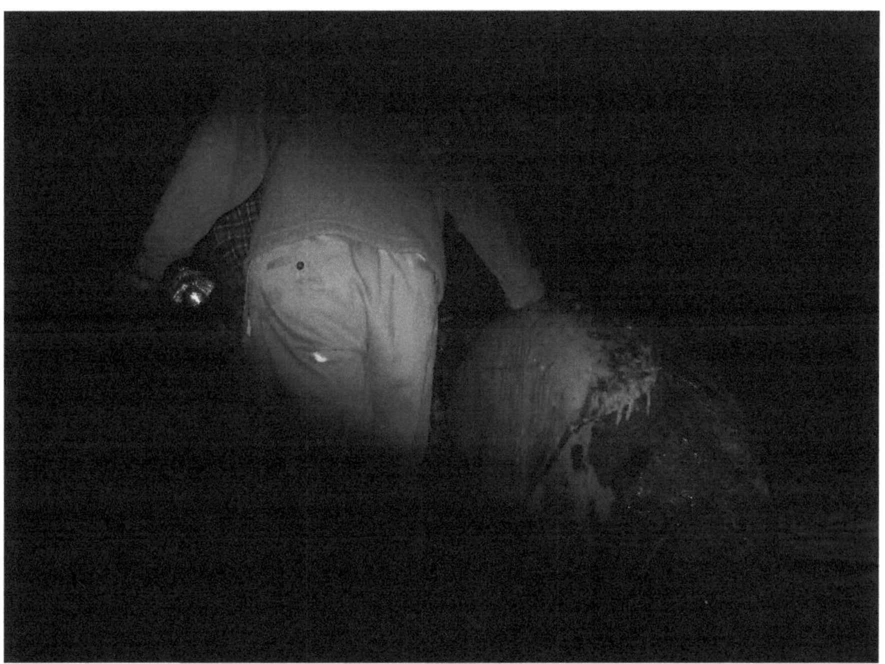

As he leans his weight out toward the leading foot, Brian flexes that part of his psyche that wants to believe in the divine. Slowly, in thoughtful increments, he studies the line of light closing between the water and his flesh. In that small space, he feels the coolness of the lake before touching down.

He teeters a moment, doubting his ability to balance between faith and flesh much longer. The dock, which he has built, is a full foot higher than the water – a flaw in the design. The big muscle in his thigh tightens (the one still planted on the dock) and the fleeting hint of a cramp wants to crawl in there between the sinewy tissues and roll around.

He extends his arms, and carefully, in a motion as delicate as Tai Chi, Brian shifts the rest of his weight off the dock. Immediately, he finds himself, for a glorious instant, standing one foot in the air, and one foot balancing on the water.

The haze that has dragged the morning in with a pall immediately evaporates, from above him a bird suddenly cries out, and the full light of sunrise throws a glare across the lake so brilliant and immortal that Brian pitches backward onto the dock and nearly knocks his head off against one of the posts supporting the long pier.

Only a moment. Not enough to say "walking" necessarily, but he has been there on that line, carried by his faith. He has been there (thank you *JesusFatherMotherMaryJoseph*) on top of the water. Across the narrow lake, there is a boy struggling to slide a canoe into the water, his thin body as white as bones. Brian watches the boy wave toward him and he wonders if the child has been a witness to this morning's miracle.

If only Beth and the children had been here to see.

I should rebuild the dock, he thinks. It was a mistake to mount it so high. Beth won't let the children out here alone, even with life jackets. What good is a lake without children?

Beth and the kids still haven't come out of the house. Beth often reminds him that it isn't a house. It is only a cabin. But he has insulated it, weather–stripped the doors and windows, installed a larger woodstove than the small pot belly that had been there when they moved in. The only similarity left to a cottage is the screened porch with its small rusty table and solitary lawn chair, the oil lamp hung in the window frame, and there in the corner, a wooden box full of jigsaw puzzles, most with pieces missing. Only the screened porch of the cabin is quaint and seasonal. For him, the rest is as robust as home. For Beth, he thinks, all of this is temporary. It is, in fact, a cabin with acreage, and with land there is always more.

Land is the thing, isn't it? he thinks. *Land defines adulthood, defines ambition, defines success.* Some of the land is brambled and twisted into impossible tangles of wildflowers and bushes, unrecognizable amalgams of trees and wiry shrubs that want to shoot as high as the horizon. Some of the property is cleared, though, and another small meadow was easily ploughed and planted with something like a prayer unrolling in his head: *JesusFatherMotherMaryJoseph*.

When they visit vineyards for research, disguised as tourists, stealing photographs of the plants, snapshots of the fruit and the trellises, Beth is always cautious, sceptical.
"Nobody grows grapes this far east or this far north," she says.
"We'll be the first," he assures, but Beth will not be convinced and would not simply believe. "Have faith," he tells her.
"I'll support you, Brian. Whatever you want to do. I will always support you; you know that." But it wasn't true. She had stopped being supportive, hadn't she? She was full of doubt, full of questions, full of her injurious adjectives and selfish pronouns. Her support for this adventure falls away too quickly to talk of *her* children and *her* life.

Brian wants to go back to another time. If only he can sustain it, everything else will follow easily. Beth is beside him in the bed and they are young and naked and they can just be here cupped together without lines, without barriers, without those strange lonesome looks they flash each other lately. Their touching bodies tangle, alive in the glory of the moment, undulating in the dance of their excitement. There are no children yet, and her skin is impossible, her mouth wet, and her beauty unfathomable. Holding on to this is more faith than walking on water.

There is a line, he thinks, like the space between his foot and the water just before he touches down, when anything is possible. *And you have to believe as you cross that line*, he thinks, *in the unexpected inevitability of all things good and glorious.*

Are they still asleep? he thinks, puzzling a little over their absence this morning.

When the children are babes, one still in diapers, Brian keeps his job in the city and the ordeal of balancing the vineyard is a tiresome commute, is full evenings and unbearable labour through exhausting weekends. Beth tends to the babies, paddles cautiously in the water close to shore, and in waning burst of encouragement, fills all of them with lemonade and smiles. When the vines are mature enough to bear fruit he quits his job.

Beth faded right away, he thinks. *As though I might outgrow this.*
"A little faith," he tells her. "This will work."
"But your job," she says, discouraged. "What about me and the kids."
"You mean *us*."

"I *mean* me and the kids."

He has been up late working on jigsaw puzzles, meticulously finishing every single one of them, carefully noting the missing pieces from each box with a circle or two marked in pencil on the lid. *If I find the pieces*, he thinks, *I can erase these marks*. Here, there is never the full picture. There is always some detail spoiled by labels, tags, notes, the name of the structure or the artist, something in the way, obstructing the perfect view of the whole image. There is always guessing with puzzles, hoping that the thing will organize itself, become obvious, apparent, or pull itself together.

Here is a puzzle, he thinks, as he hikes back up from the lake, a pair of deerflies tracing a confusion around his head. *When do you know when to move on?* Brian trails across the yard away from the cabin and down toward the field. Here is the barn that Brian built. There is a line crossing the path, a wire, or a shank of thin, thin rope that he does not recognize tracing through the dirt and grass. *Here is a puzzle*. He stops with the toe of his sandal stepping across the cord.
This time, he speaks out loud. "What is this doing here?"

He looks back up toward the house expecting to see Beth and the children in the bay window smiling, laughing at the lark at having laid this line here for no particular reason except to arouse his attention. The bay window is dark, the cabin a dead hulk across the yard. *They have slept so late*, he thinks. There is something like a prayer for them he mumbles: *JesusFatherMotherMaryJoseph*, he says inside, and then out loud: Keep them."

Brian can't remember letting go. He cannot remember when the little changes happened, when he constructed the algebra that has added up to this. He waves away the flies, but they will not be discouraged. There are only the little changes, aren't there? The iterations that repeat, shift, repeat, shift, until you find yourself in a place, as a thing you don't recognize.

He turns toward the field, his foot still stepping on the line in the sparse grass which he feels through the sandal as sharply as a stone. The trellises stretch beyond a rise in wide rows. *Rows of promise*, he thinks. *When the fruit comes*, he thinks, *everything else will follow easily*. Brian lines up Beth and the two children in a gentle row at Christmas and sets the camera to take their picture. He rushes over to be in the picture with them. Instead, he trips and spills over the Christmas tree knocking everything out of place. What a strange picture the camera takes: all of them are turned away reaching to rescue the tree and Beth looks toward him with supreme, nearly absolute disappointment. He lines them up again to take the right picture, but this one never makes it to a frame. Even the small change retains the dishonesty of the previous moment with Beth's face twisted in despair.

A June bug panics in a too early flight. Brian watches the thing fall from the air and land against a patch of bare ground in front of the barn, its wings like fingernails thrumming aimlessly against the clay casting a huff of dust around it. *I hope I'm not late*, he thinks. Spring seems to have already rolled in full of glory, while he pauses here, stands with his foot on a strange line and the rows of grapevine stretching forever. There is so much to do. There is fertilizer to move from the barn, trellises to patch and vines to pare down. Brian remembers the old tractor and the hydraulic line that burst during the last snow. Brian remembers the tractor parked behind the barn in need of repair.

String is for tying around a finger to remember. String is for holding things together when they want to come apart. Brian moves to the barn and swings the small door wide. This is not much of a barn. *Shed* is too modest a name, but *barn* somehow too ambitious. The tractor was meant to fit inside, but the whole project has come together wrong. There might have been a stall for a horse, or a loft, for climbing up into. He should have built this differently, but the time and the money were never enough. *When the harvest starts paying, then I will build a real barn*, he thinks. *Then Beth will see that this is something real. Then she will see that there is no point in walking away. There are always options*, Brian thinks. *You just need to believe.*

Somewhere in the barn, a chipmunk whistles erratically, insulted by Brian's interruption.

"What do we need all that fertilizer for?" she says.
"For the plants," he says.
"And the diesel?"
"For the tractor."
"It's too much," she says. "Can you afford it?"
"You always say that," he says. "We'll be fine."

Brian struggles suddenly, spinning in the spider web logic of his morning. *Why are they not already awake chasing down to the barn in their rubber boots and dungarees? Has something happened?*

Brian traces the yellow line of cord with his eyes. It snakes behind the cans of diesel and bags of fertilizer.

Has something happened? he thinks. *Why are they not awake?*

He feels sweat overwhelming his brow and dripping down his face. Brian reaches into his pocket for a rag. He always has a rag. Instead, he opens his fist to a lighter. "I don't smoke," he says.

What have I done? he thinks, trying to remember everything before the miracle. There is something like a prayer thundering in him: *JesusFatherMotherMaryJoseph what have I done?*

Brian flexes that part of his psyche that wants to accept the redemption of the divine but there is something like a cramp sliding in there between the flesh and the faith.

I made a list, he thinks. *Didn't I make a list? I always have a list.*

He digs into the other pocket and pulls out a folded recipe card. He has enough things to do buzzing around his head to fill a notebook: lines of chores and things undone that want for a string tied around a finger. This card is all he can find last night when he sits to plan. There are two things on the list that have already been crossed out. *Blotted* is a better word – worked and reworked with a pencil twisting little circles so that the two lines are unreadable and the card is bruised with the rubbing over it. They are gone and he can't even remember them. The third thing is about the water, and Brian searches his other pockets for a nub of pencil, but there is nothing else in there. Number four is this thing with the lighter. Number five is a number with a tiny period of a dot beside it. He doesn't remember what number five is to be, but he believes that it will come to him as soon as he gets through number four. After he gets through number four, everything else will come easily.

There had been a dream last night, he thinks: *Children laughing between trees, telling me to wake up and come along as though there was something to be missed if I waited.* Brian thinks of the boy across the lake and wonders if he was really waving or beckoning.

Brian closes the barn door and crouches outside by the end of the yellow line traced through the dull grass. The lighter takes three strikes to light, but the cord catches easily and burns with a chasing spark. He feels heat rising in himself, the want to slow things down while somehow being pulled strenuously onward. *How do you know*, he thinks, *when it's time to move on? How does Beth figure out something like that? Here is a puzzle with too many missing pieces; if only I had a pencil to mark them down*, he thinks. Absently, he squeezes the recipe card in his fist. He leans his weight first on one foot and then the other, moving slightly closer toward the barn, and steals another look over his shoulder to the empty bay window to see if anyone is watching. He thinks of

the thin bony boy on the lake with his canoe and wonders if he will be a
witness. For Brian, there is something like a prayer choking him, yet he
cannot speak the words. There is a glorious moment of thunderous silence,
and then, just as suddenly, Brian feels himself lifted up, and impossibly filled
with light.

Harvest first appeared in Queen's Quarterly in the spring of 2011. The story was
nominated for the National Magazine Award in the fiction category and was
anthologized in a short run collection edited by Helen Humphrey. In the summer
of 2010, I attended a writing workshop north of Kingston where Helen was the
writer-in-residence for the week-long event. I had been working on the character
and a rough plot line prior to the workshop. She gave the writers an assignment
which brought the story together. I had given it a different title; Ms. Humphrey
suggested Harvest. Of course, I followed her wisdom.

I had been sending stories out for several years with no success. At the time, I was
so naïve about publishing, When I finished writing this piece, I wanted to call it
quits. I sent this story to a different Canadian publication where it was quickly
turned down. Queen's Quarterly, I was certain, was out of reach for me. I gambled
and sent them the story. I cried when they emailed an acceptance letter.

The story received some feedback from a reader who sent me a note questioning
the hopelessness of the tale. Other readers asked me if Brian had killed his family.
The truth is that I don't see it as a hopeless story, nor do I know where his family
is. Beginnings come in variety of ways.

At first, it felt very nearly comical. I might even have exclaimed, "Oh, dear!" Not in some grave way, but lightly, as though someone had dropped the pie just before dessert. I noticed the blanket first, fluttering up over our heads and then off the back of the ferry, but then the baby, like a stone, cartwheeled, hit the railing on the deck below us, and disappeared into the black.

Of course, I was the first to jump in, diving, shouting, choking. Others joined me. I am not a strong swimmer. The ferry circled around. Ropes were launched, hooks, lifebuoys. Something clocked me in the head and I have a scar where eight stitches were neatly tied. When they pulled me back in, someone asked what happened. I reasoned that it was the batting in his clothing, at once thick enough to keep him warm and yet suddenly a sponge heavy enough to drown him. He was barely a month old, not even strong enough to gasp, or fight.

The baby might just as well have been a stone, he sank so quickly. The body was never recovered. Whispers spread that he was unwanted, that we had perhaps killed him in some more sinister fashion and buried the body in the garden behind the house, or fed his flesh to dogs. Of course, it wasn't true. That sort of talk just happens. I had seen his face only moments before the ferry lurched and Janine, *tragic girl*, stumbled. It was an accident, simple and cruel.

"Do you think it's ironic," she asked, "that we named him Jonah?"

"We live on an island," I told her. "Jonah is a perfectly common seafaring name."

"What other seafaring names might we have called him?"

"I don't know," I said. "After Jonah there is…" But I can't think of any.

"You see?"

"It's a perfectly common name. There is nothing ironic about it. I expect that if we went down to the park where the children are playing and launched ten pebbles into the air, we would hit three Jonahs."

"You would throw stones at children to prove a point?" She smiled, a rare, beautiful thing.

We never held a funeral or held a memorial service. In the first few months after the ferry tragedy, rumours spread about Janine's madness. Before his first birthday, our social circle dwindled to just Janine, myself, and the memory of Jonah. Janine didn't get lonely as I did.

He stayed with us. In the beginning, Janine spoke with him, but then I fell into the game. We lay in bed together with a small pillow tucked between us to hold his place. She would sing him a song and urge a nursery rhyme from me. After a while, the pillow disappeared, and there was only the small space between us. Sometimes I would come home from work and find her in full conversation babbling away with him. She would hand him to me and I would oblige, sometimes gesture as though he had gained weight since yesterday. Together we would change his diaper.

Jonah was nearly two when Janine brought home a small toothbrush. She hummed with him while they brushed, cloistered together behind the bathroom door. Afterwards, I would find the toothbrush wet, sitting next to mine in the cup on the shelf. Almost ten years passed before I had the courage to throw the thing out. It was well worn, too, and I couldn't figure if she was brushing her thumb, the side of the sink, or her own teeth with it. She asked me about where it had gone, I shrugged, made the excuse that it was old, and then replaced it with a larger, adult toothbrush.

I never did ask her to stop. I participated. I talked with him. I could never tell her how jealous he made me because he occupied so much of her time. I wanted her to myself, but first I wanted her happy.

One morning when Jonah was barely five, she was at the door with a bag, towels, and a picnic lunch.

"Where are you going?"

"I'm going to the beach," she said. "I'm going to teach him how to swim so that he doesn't drown." I waited for her to say, "*again*," but instead that face appeared, the face only the saddest mothers ever wear, a look no one dare contradict or appease.

"I'll go with you," I said quickly, anxious not to lose her, and hurried to get myself a towel and trunks.

She was no better a swimmer than I, but she would push further than I ever could, out beyond the breakers and into the swells. I always fell back and she never would listen to me imploring her to turn around. By the time I reached the shore, she was barely a dot on the horizon. Sometimes the spray from a passing humpback gave the impression that there was someone out there with her splashing around. I fooled myself into believing that I could hear her laughter over the sound of the sea and wind. It was true though. She was alive out there, laughing, full of vigour and energy. After the swim, we would always drive home without words. After each swim, Janine was nearly catatonic with joy. I could not break her mood or her silence. At home, she would rush to his room and sit there well into the evening. Quietly, she would stare into one space, as though he was fixed there looking back at her. I would retire to the carport to smoke and brood.

She insisted on teaching him how to cook and knit, so I had to teach him to make a birdhouse and sharpen a pocket knife. By that point, he had his own knife that I carried for him. He was a handsome teenager. He wasn't like the other island boys, skulking around, nervous with angst, noisy for no reason at all. He read ferociously, sometimes two and three books at a time. I think Janine made the librarian uncomfortable with her borrowing habits. Maybe it was the confession that the books were for Jonah. The whole island had disintegrated into polite acceptance of Janine and me. Jonah learned chess and played quite a challenging game. For a while, he tried to talk Janine into letting him sail, but she wouldn't have it. "Why can't you be happy sitting at home with us?"

One night, when he was older, I asked Jonah, "Do you want me to teach you how to smoke?" I lit a second cigarette. "Now, I'll hold it for you because if mother finds stains on your fingers, I'm a dead man." I believe Jonah laughed with me that night.

I had the sense that he wanted to go, to grow up, but Janine refused to accept the change in him. "He is still so young," she confided to me one night while we lay in bed. It had been years since he'd moved to his own room; still the little space between us persisted like a cramp.

"Janine, he's restless. It's time to let him go."

"How can you be so thoughtless," she snapped. "He's my baby. I don't have to let him go."

"You can hold him too tightly, you know."

She turned her back to me and feigned sleep. I crawled out of the bed.

"Where are you going?"

"Downstairs for a glass of water."

She knew this as my code for smoking.

He had been out ahead of me. I could smell the cigarette freshly smoked below the slant of the carport roof. "You won't have a second one from me tonight," I told him. "You've got your mother all upset with your growing."

He had been dead for more than twenty years. I nearly lost count. Janine stopped celebrating his birthday soon after he turned twelve. She knew he was older, but didn't want to accept he was becoming a man.

One morning I couldn't find my shoes.

"Jonah must have worn them to work," Janine said.

"He has a job now?"

"He hired on with one of the fishing boats."

"That's dangerous work."

"He'll be okay," she said. "He knows how to swim, remember? I taught him."

"I remember," I said and kissed her. "I should buy him proper boots for the job."

"That would be kind," she said and threw her arms around my neck. "You are a good father." When she pulled away, Janine had tears in her eyes. "I'm not ready to let him go."

"I know," I said. "You'll know when it's time." I didn't dare ask her where she had hidden my shoes. It might only cost me a pair of boots to get them back.

Janine announces that Jonah called and is working late. We have the evening alone. We cross to the city with the car and drive to Burnham Street to a restaurant that has been there since our youth.

"I love you," I tell her.

"I know," she says, her thoughts somewhere else, maybe on the ferry or the weather, which seems uneasy, gloomy.

We hold hands and browse the stores and galleries up Melville Road, and then along Peddler's Way, a pedestrian market where I first kissed Janine when we were young. When everything closes we window shop instead. We would have had a different life in the city, but it isn't worth mentioning. I am so happy to be with her like this. When I finally check the time, it's already too late and we have missed the last ferry home. We drive quickly to the harbour just the same, in case the service is also late. Janine points to the lights in the bay where the ferry is already twenty minutes out.

"Look," she says. "There is a trawler down at the other end of the pier. They look about ready to cast off. Do you think they'd give us passage home?"

"I don't think they are allowed to take passengers."

She grabs my hand and starts pulling me down the boardwalk. "Let's try," she says.

"We can stay in town," I tell her. "I'll pay for a hotel."

"Nonsense," she says, breathless from jogging. "If we're lucky, it'll be Jonah's boat." She waves at a crewman stowing ropes and gear in the front hold. He waves back, clearly uncertain about who we are. We slow a little as we approach. "You ask him, Tom, you ask if they'll take us for the trip. Maybe that man knows Jonah."

"I'll ask," I say to her, then stop to meet her sad, empty eyes. "But I won't worry the captain by asking about his crew."

She looks at me for a minute and I'm not sure what she is thinking. Finally, she smiles. "You're a clever one, Tom. We wouldn't want to get Jonah in trouble for having family on board."

The first crewman I talk to, the one stowing the ropes, doesn't know what to say to my request, so he calls another over. This one signals to the pilot house and the captain leans out to see what the trouble is. I have to shout above the din of the engines to be heard, but he waves us aboard. I can tell we are an annoyance for him. The young sailor, now promoted to porter or yeoman, leads us to a small open passageway between the portside railing and the pilot house.

"There is a storm coming," he tells us. "We're going to moor in the lee side of the island." He walks away from us before I can ask if there is a better place for Janine and I should the storm strike.

The sea is already rough, and I'm afraid that Janine will panic. She holds me tightly and presses her head against my shoulder. I can feel her heart beating next to mine and I think this is the most romantic evening we've shared in many years.

Halfway across the bay, a terrible crack draws both our attention to the back of the boat. I watch as a bolt of heavy netting tumbles off and unravels into the sea. Apparently, some part of the rigging has snapped. Two sailors rush to the scene. The first unsheathes a machete and is about the cut the dragging equipment free when the other yells to him and points overboard. The machete disappears and suddenly both men are tugging at the netting. Two strange hands appear on the low stern railing from the darkness. Then arms climb over into the boat. Suddenly, there is a young man, wet and shivering beside the others, struggling to stand. I take him to be a crewman who was pushed overboard by the failed equipment. I feel Janine stiffen and I know she has something else in mind. I can feel the impending horror of the storm rolling below us.

"Jonah," she cries out. Remarkably, the young man looks up at her. Before I can catch her, she is gone. I watch her wrap herself around him. I believe she means to land an embrace, but instead, the strange couple pitch silently overboard.

Hooks, ropes, and lifebuoys are thrown into the fray. Lights and horns blare. More sailors spill onto the deck from below. I am frozen in the scene, unable to comprehend what has just occurred. Before long, the crew have the netting attached to a winch and the mess is slowly wound back into the boat. And then there are two bodies resting on the deck wrapped in a prison of knots. She did not fight, did not let go. Instead, she pinned his arms down, and they drowned together. I imagine her whispering to him in the moments before they hit the water. "This is not your world, Jonah. If you enter it like this, you will only die over and over again."

There are two spaces in the bed beside me. There is a small pillow for Jonah, who is little again. A slightly larger pillow stands in for Janine. I lean over and kiss them both and wish them goodnight. In the morning, I will make her a breakfast of soft boiled eggs and toast. Perhaps there will be a chance for me to feed her while she nurses the baby.

Against an All Blue Sky appeared in The Cold Creek Review in the summer of 2017. I can think of no worse horror than losing a child. This story taught me that there is something worse – the inability to heal. Of all the characters I've written, I think that this couple are the saddest and most desperate.

The sofa has been here almost since the beginning. I pull my knees up, hug them close to me, and listen to my father apologize before he shoves the end of a dull, black handgun into his mouth. I don't hear the blast. Instead, it is my mother's voice as she comes rushing in from the kitchen – *Why? Why? Why?* – Louder every time; her olive skin turns nearly purple from screaming.

The very next week, we empty the apartment because she can't afford this one anymore. That's what she tells me. But we only load our belongings onto the elevator down from the fourteenth floor to the sixth. Of course, I don't ask her about it, nor do I point out that the new apartment is exactly the same as the old one except that I can't see the lake from the balcony. It's the first thing I find missing. We make more than a dozen trips up and down the elevator carrying garbage bags full of belongings, mattresses, chairs, tables, armfuls of dishes and Tupperware, then a grocery cart – the one from the lobby – full of food. The landlord and his son are the only help we have since Mom's family lives out of town and Dad's family is grieving so hard they can't make the ten minutes to come over and help.

I stand in the doorway of the apartment and I look into the little hole where the bolt from the door lands. This one time, before I was tall enough to see inside the cavity, I dropped my chewing gum down inside the hole. I wonder how many little boys before me dropped chewing gum or candy or army men or bits of eraser down inside the metal door frame, if only to imagine where the object might land, if it lands at all. I think that there is probably a time capsule's worth of debris down there: the secret stash of curious children stranded in this doorway, pondering, waiting, worrying.

There's only one thing left in the apartment and it's the sofa. Mom tugs at my arm and tells me it's time to go.

What about the sofa?

We're leaving it here.

But we have to bring it with us. It's ours.

It's dirty, she says, Now, come on. We have to unpack downstairs.

I tell myself that there is nothing really packed, so I don't know what the big deal is. The big deal here is that the sofa is alone and needs to come with us.

It's not that dirty.

We're leaving it. Now come on.

I'm going to stay here a while, then. If that's okay.

There is a moment before she loosens the tension on my arm when I think she won't let me stay. I can't look at her because I know that we will have to say more things to each other and I'm not ready for that yet. I'm still only seven years old.

Don't be long, she says, and I watch her from behind as she moves down toward the elevator carrying our electric frying pan under her arm and smoking a cigarette.

At first, I can't just walk into the apartment. Empty like this, it's a place I'm not used to. I focus on the sofa and suddenly I can imagine the table to one side of it, with a lamp, and in front of it there once was a rug. But that disappeared right away. There is a painting on the wall, a landscape from K-Mart; the shapes and colours in the painting match the mottled pattern on the sofa. I can't accurately decipher for myself its complex swirls and shapes, sometimes fruit, sometimes vessels wrapped and scrolled with vines and intersecting vegetation. Orange. Brown. Orange. Red. Brown. Black. Yellow. And then orange again. It's like that story about the illustrated man where his tattoos, his markings, tell you something different each time you look. The sofa is not defined by the pattern or even the colours so much as just an impression of itself, it introduces itself: furniture overwhelmed by confusion. When the room presents itself full like this, I cross the hollowness of it and land on the sofa. I'm wearing shorts and the rough, dry fabric is scratchy against my skin. I pull my legs up and hug them to me. Mom isn't really concerned with the dirt. Not the crusty place where my sister spilled her macaroni and cheese. Not the places where someone fell asleep and drooled. She isn't even worried about the ratty patch where our butts have worn one cushion nearly bare. There are tiny flecks of him spattered along the front of the sofa. I know this because I had to wash some of the flecks off of my skin.

It isn't very long before she's in the doorway calling me to her.
It's time, she says. I need your help.
We can't leave it, I tell her.
It's not coming.
I don't know how to argue with her because she says everything so *finally*.
But, we can't leave it.
Come on, Frank.
No.
I am not bringing that thing into our new home.
We can't sit on the floor.
We'll get a new one.
I thought you didn't have any money.
It's old.
When I am old, will you leave me behind?
Come now. Please, Frank. Please.
I like *this* one.

Before she says anything else, I hear the elevator ding and then open. The landlord and his son are in the hallway, their voices echo like they might in a hospital or an asylum. He talks to Mom who finally lowers her head. He wants to charge her to throw the sofa into the dumpster, but he'll move it down to the new place for free. I should have never tried to argue with her because I know it has only made this worse.
As the elevator closes with the landlord and his son tucked in there neatly with the sofa, Mom and I wait for the next one. I'm sorry, I tell her, but she only squeezes my hand sadly.
We could put plastic on it, like on Gramma's sofa, I say, so that it doesn't get any dirtier.

We never cover it, not even with a blanket. For the longest time, the furniture, even the painting, occupy the new apartment in the same exact layout as in the old place. Only the carpet and the view of the lake are missing. Either Mom doesn't notice, or it doesn't matter anymore.

Mom is close and she has an arm around me. I think I'm eleven. There's a small ceramic ashtray on the arm of the sofa. It's full, but she's still smoking. When she exhales, I draw short convulsive breaths so that I can share the disease. I think we will be closer because of it. I think she mistakes my stilted, erratic breathing for crying, so she draws her body down the length of the sofa and holds me tighter, closer, so that I won't fall off. I feel the softness of her breast, the warmth of her belly, and the steady rhythm of her diaphragm lifting and falling. I hear the unsteady drumming of her heart and see the sweat dampening her neck. She bends her one leg, draws her knee up, and the bottom of me rests in the space she creates. I begin to tremble, her breath, the smell of cigarettes, is hot on my face and she grips me so tightly I think that if I do not breathe, then the trembling will go away. This is a moment my body never forgets.

It's okay to be lonely, she says. Everybody is lonely.

Does it go away?

I don't think it ever does, she says. I think about finding another man, but I don't think I would stop being empty.

I'm thirteen and Mom is at one end and I'm at the other. She hands me a cigarette. I have my own ashtray. I have one of her glasses and I am chewing the ice cubes. The little bit of liquid in the glass tastes like the smell of old leaves. It's warm in my throat, hot in my belly. My one hand is down between the cushion and the arm of the sofa. There's something down there, a string, or a necklace maybe. I leave it there. I think of the opening in Dad's skull, the dripping from the ceiling, the scar that I dream about so often, rushing to him in dream-speed, trying to hold it closed, trying to wrap the cotton rug around his head so that he'll stop bleeding. Squeezing and squeezing so that he'll be okay. It didn't really happen that way. I just sat there holding my legs, swaying, trying to stay focussed on the TV. Mom hands me leftover ice cubes all the time and sometimes there's more than enough of the old leaves to warm my belly and cloud my head.

Hold me, she says, and I slide across the rough fabric and she rocks me against her and I feel ashamed because of what my body does and how sick I feel in her arms.

He's going to hell, you know. She whispers.

How can you know that?

It's where people go who can't be redeemed.

Can I go with him?

She doesn't answer me; we never talk about him again.

My sister is too young to remember. I think that she pissed her pants when it happened. She was sitting right beside me at the time. When she is fifteen, I come home and find Karen and her boyfriend on the sofa. He turns towards me and I see his penis dangling there, over her. He looks at me stupidly, an animal suddenly stranded in headlights. I'm captivated by the hollow her buttocks makes in the cushion, a dark, forbidden depression. Suddenly, like kites, they fly off to the bedroom where I hear her swearing and him laughing. Not long after that, she moves out, pregnant, to the boyfriend's apartment.

There are things that I remember but more that I forget. I haven't seen either of them, Mom or Karen, in such a long time. Mom disappeared, and Karen just never calls anymore. I know where she is; she and the boyfriend rent a trailer down there next to the lake. The summers might be pleasant, but I'm sure the winters are hell. Mom never stops drinking. She held enough ice cubes out to me so that the lines blurred into nothing I can recognize. When I move out of the sixth floor apartment, I'm the only one left. The one thing I take with me is the sofa.

From the basement where I rent now, I can't see the lake, or any of the buildings that sprawl the city. I can see a bit of grass and it makes me smile to think I am almost half buried, closer than I might otherwise get while I'm still conscious. When Mom came unglued, I don't think she knew anything. She's not dead. I don't think so. But, I think she's with Dad in a lot of ways. I have trouble explaining it. I'm done. I have trouble explaining that one too. Fortunately, there's nobody to explain it to. I'm not sure what my sister tells her kid. Maybe he's not old enough yet. I wonder if he's eight or nine now. I don't remember meeting him.

Outside of my door, there's a concrete well, a sort of landing where I might keep a bicycle or a hibachi. I have neither. The stairs go up and out into the yard. I stand in the doorway and stick my finger into the little hole where the door bolts tight. I touch something soft and that makes me smile too. There's nothing left in the apartment except the sofa; I've pawned everything else. That's what you do when you're desperate. I saw it on TV.

You can tell me, I expect: This is the lunatic fringe, right? The place people go to when they figure out there's no such thing as heaven, no such thing as hell, and redemption is only is the lie that revenge tries to tell you. There isn't a lot that makes sense to me anymore. Mom was right about one thing, though: Lonely never goes away. It just grows and grows until it's tight on you like a tourniquet and I can only suck little breaths through the jaundiced filter of half-smoked cigarettes.

I drag the old sofa, heavy as an anchor, up the stairs and into the yard. I can see a few people already out on their balconies looking down at me. I have a flask of rye and I pour it all out over the fabric. People have been burning their important things forever, right? Making sacrifices of one kind or another. This is the only thing I have left, so here it is, stains and all. The first match doesn't catch and someone up there laughs and I hear beer bottles clink against a metal railing. The second match keeps and I drop it onto the cushion. The flash of light shoves me back and the thing woofs like a big, bad dog and the breath of it steals the air from all around the blaze. There are so many faces in the smoke and the flames: most of them I don't recognize, but my father smiles at me. The sirens draw more people outside onto their balconies. Some of the children sneak onto the fire escape to get closer. I drop back into the shadows, down the concrete well, and into my small room. I have no furniture now, so I just stand here looking down at the place where the boy in me used to sit. I suppose that something in the burning says that I am a man now, the glass having gone all dark instead of clear.

A Very Small Stain was accepted for publication and appeared in the University of San Francisco's online literary magazine Switchback in the spring of 2013.

I'm fascinated by Shakespeare's character Hamlet. Like many of the bard's characters, Hamlet has to come to terms with his own tragic flaw. Arguably, this premise is the beginning of all great characters. The character in this story is my Hamlet, a man who divides and divides until he finds the lowest common denominator. There's a tiny bit of hope at the end and an homage to the famous quote (apparently oft misattributed to John Wesley), "I set myself on fire and they come to watch me burn." Of course, nobody believes that this character will eventually be anything other than a man living on the streets without a sofa.

The bearings in the ceiling fan rattle, an old man with loose dentures.
"Tom, you oughta get up there and oil that thing."

Shay drops a plate in front of me: two eggs, toast, and a small puddle of sour relish. Ten years on, she still looks as good as a bride.

"Had another dream about Lucy," I tell her.

He hit me without slowing his hand as it struck. But I took it. I stood there and took it, and little Lucy watched. The horror I always dream about Lucy is about her and Pa. He was mean, especially drunk. In the dream, he's looking at her wrong. He always looked at her wrong. Even at eight years old, I think it's possible to have an instinct for something like that. She wasn't quite three – not old enough to defend herself against a monster. Like a dog, I slept on her floor. She would look down on me and in her very little voice she would whisper, "You okay?" I would flutter my eyelids once for "yes" even if it felt like two for "no." Sometimes she would lean down from her bed and offer butterfly kisses to the bruises on my back and shoulders.

"Maybe you should call her," Shay says. "Dreams are omens when they're about people you love. Your sister might be in trouble."

"Of course, she's in trouble. That bastard could do better than a trailer park for her and Bird."

"She loves him, Tom. Maybe she doesn't want more than what he has to offer."

"She can do better is all I'm saying."

"Maybe you coulda done better than a loudmouth like me." Shay smiles and bumps my chair as she passes to the sink. I suppose I should rush and hug her, grab her ass, and growl something clever, but it's not in me right now. I'm too anxious about Lucy and Bird.

Bird is six. Autism. There's no school program for him out where she lives, so she has to care for him full-time and then try to live off of the boy's disability cheques. She calls it *homeschooling* but it's really just despair. He's a good kid. He doesn't get into trouble or run off. He's not hyper, but he's not a math genius or anything like that. He repeats things. Sometimes Bird will hear something and like it so much he'll repeat it for days afterwards. Lucy took a hate to me calling him Parrot. She thought it was cruel. "He's not a bird," she said. *Bird* stuck. He doesn't respond to it any more than he responds to *Andrew*, but Bird works for Lucy. When I muss his shock of white-blond hair, he clamps his hand on mine and announces, "Bird."

Her husband, Dice, came along after the baby. Dice isn't his real name any more than Bird fits Andrew. I call Bird to his face and Dice to his face. Bird doesn't mind. Dice sneers but doesn't correct to Ryan. I'm not sure Dice even knows that Bird is really Andrew. Not that it would matter. Dice was a risk from the beginning. Brainless poster boy. He runs like he's fifteen and respects Lucy about the same. He isn't much for being a dad. Dice is big and meaty, a bouncer at the strip club out by the airport. He was somebody once, a fullback for a farm team, but never made the draft. Now the bulk only serves to hustle drunks aside or push Lucy around.

I think about killing him. All the time it's on my mind. He's bigger than the refrigerator in their tiny home and he spends everything he makes on steroids and beer so that they never get ahead. I planned a fishing trip for a chance to drown him, but I never could convince Shay or Lucy to rent a place up in the Northlands. Too many bugs, they both said. It was just as well. I wasn't sure that Dice wouldn't drown me first.

Eventually, fate caught up with Pa and he was locked up, but Lucy went strange without him around. She started seeing boys before she wore a training bra. She was having sex that early, I'm sure. I had trouble loving her, liking her, or caring about her during those early years. I resented that she was weak. She was lonely for all the wrong ones, and I wasn't much help for her, couldn't stop her from running the wrong game. She had two cleaned out before she finished high school but when she got pregnant the third time, they wouldn't take it out of her, so she was stuck. I suspect Lucy did something to herself, which is why Bird came out wrong, but I've never asked or said it to anyone. Since Bird came along, she's settled down and I can look out for her again. I suppose things come around the way you want them to if you wait long enough. Maybe I think the old man's teeth flapping above our heads will fix themselves and Shay just needs to be more patient.

"Earth to Tom," Shay says. "Where'd you go?"

"Tired, I guess."

"You're worrying about Lucy and Bird, aren't you?"

"Maybe." I scoop egg and relish on a crust of toast and listen to the radio hum on the windowsill. Tammy Wynnette is working her drowsy way through *Stand by Your Man*. It's an old song, one Pa used to like. I think poor Tammy never met a guy like Dice, or Pa.

"You know, Tom, you're just a sack of assorted troubles held together by a decent man. If you don't stop obsessing about Dice, it's going to destroy the good man and the rest of you will just fall to pieces."

"I gotta work," I tell her. "I'm glad you take care of me, Shay."

I kiss her, drag the service jacket on, check that my belt is on right, and that the holster is fastened shut. I clip the walkie in place and adjust the volume for the mic buttoned to my shoulder. Shay smiles coyly.

"What is it?"

"I'll never get over how good you look in that uniform. That jacket makes you twice as big as you are, and that's not just your size I'm talking about."

"You must be thinking about some other man, Shay. I don't feel anything more in this outfit than weighed down by the job. I'd rather be here eating toast and eggs all morning than dealing with what waits for me out there."

Hamlin's Creek is not a bad town. It's just been forgotten. Over the years, I've held a whole line of sales jobs. I sold fast food, clothes, vacuum cleaners (door-to-door), peddled credit card accounts in the entrance to the mall, and even took a two-year business program at community college. That one set me up with a job as advertising manager at the local television station. After a year, I lost the urge. Police training was the last thing in the world I wanted to do, but Shay said I had energy to help people. She said I was good with people. And besides, the pay was more than double what I'd made at any other job.

If I invited Dice out hunting, I could shoot him square in the back and make it look like an accident. Of course, the setup would have to be perfect. If I only hurt him, that would be no good. He'd either turn on me and kill me, or be a burden to Lucy that she couldn't afford.

The patrol car smells like a hobo convention and I'm sure the back seat has seen more piss and vomit than I ever want to clean up. Before clocking in for my shift, I ride out to Lucy's to make sure she's okay. I tried to convince her to move with Bird to an apartment in town. Where she lives is isolated. Dice will never have enough of anything to move them up.

We've been going through a cold spell which might be all we get of winter this year. Shay suggests phoning, but I'd rather see her in the real. Sometimes Bird sits outside the trailer in the yard and draws patterns in the dirt with a stick and rocks back and forth with abandon. Today, he's sitting in his other favourite spot at the little dining table which also doubles as the TV room. Above his head is the one kitchen cupboard used for dishes. Across the table from Bird, there might once have been more cupboards, but Dice hung a little TV there instead. Lucy told me that Dice clocks his head every time he sits down and they spend the rest of the night listening to Bird swear a repetitive blue streak at them. It might be funny if it weren't so awful.

"Hi Bird," I say to him.
"Hi Bird," he repeats without looking at me. He has a colouring book in front of him with a few crayons, but he doesn't touch them. The TV is broken and only has one volume which is loud. I don't recognize the animated characters, but it doesn't seem that Bird minds them very much. "Hi Bird," he says again.
Lucy comes out from the bedroom.
"Your screen door has a busted hinge," I tell her. She moves close and hugs me. She still smells like sleep. "Where's Dice?"
"He's up to the store. We're out of coffee."
Lucy is wearing a thin nightgown, the long, draping kind a much older woman might wear. I catch a fresh hand-sized welt on her bare arm. She sees me notice, swings briskly back into the bedroom and grabs a cardigan. She looks even older buried in the ratty sweater.
"He's still hitting you." I make it a pronouncement rather than a question. She's not likely to answer a question straight, and we're family, so a cold truth is always better than a lukewarm lie.
"He's still hitting you," Bird sings.
"Hush and watch your show," Lucy tells him hard.
"He's still hitting you," Bird says again.
"Look at that, Tommy." She slaps her thigh, suddenly frustrated and points an angry finger at me. "Dice'll come home and hear that and then where will I be?"
I think of her little butterfly kisses. "You're welcome to come live with Shay and me. You know that, right?"

"You say that every damn time. I don't need to leave here. This is my home."

"Every damn time," Bird echoes. Lucy gives me a look to burn.

"When you're ready to get out, I just want you to know there's a safe place for you."

"I'm safe here," she says. She wants to say more, something about how he's not that bad, or that he's actually good to her sometimes, but she knows better, knows that I won't believe any defence or excuse she makes for him. She also knows better than to cast lukewarm lies at me. "I forgot to get coffee when I went shopping yesterday. That's all. I deserved it." She touches the bruises on her arm through the sweater. "Do you want a glass of water?"

"I'm not a guest, Lucy. I'm family. If I want a glass of water I think that I could help myself. And nobody deserves what you get from him." I don't know why I'm angry with her. "I came to check on you is all, came to make sure you weren't dead."

"Make sure you weren't dead," Bird says. He picks up a blue crayon in a tight little fist and scribbles randomly on the page, skipping over the shapes and the lines as though they weren't there at all. Lucy busies herself with the few dishes in the sink.

"I've got to get to work, Lucy. Call if you need me. The station will patch you right through to me."

The door whines when I leave and I know Dice won't do anything to fix it, that I'll have to be at that job for her.

As I ready to back the cruiser up, the world shifts while I am stopped, the steady click from the turn signal bounces around my head. In that moment, in that shift, Dice races by and I can't understand why he flies past the trailer park. I hurry to catch up and settle in behind his Camaro until we're away from the town. He's cheating on Lucy. It's the only logical explanation. He's headed further out from town to service one of the girls from the club, or maybe an old girlfriend. I can see his eyes in his rear view. He's sizing me up, threatening me by slowing and then speeding away. I think he's laughing at me. I throw on the cherries, but he doesn't take me seriously. I add the scream of the siren and he still doesn't stop. This is the big one. This is it. I lay my foot solid on the ground and haul up on his bumper hard enough to pull his back end up off the road. Both cars lurch, but it's Dice's car that doesn't respond to the driver's commands. Instead, the rocket launches across the oncoming traffic lane, rolls once down into the ditch and slams into a tree about half as wide as the Camaro. I watch his body flip-flop out through the shattered windshield and land motionless in the short, dry grass.

Then I am back outside the trailer, the click of the turn signal the only steady thing I can focus on. Lucy is in the doorway holding Bird on her hip. His body is nearly as long as she is tall but she still holds him like he is an infant. She wants to smile, but I think she's forgotten how. Dice is still alive somewhere out on the county road chasing coffee or a six pack or a carton of smokes oblivious to the imagined carnage in my head. The com on my shoulder crackles and reminds me I'm supposed to be on duty. I blow a kiss out the window to my sister and head back towards Hamlin's Creek.

***

"How was your day?" Shay asks. She takes the jacket from me and plants a kiss hard against my lips.

"Fine," I say.

"Did you see Lucy this morning?"

"Ya."

"She okay?"

"Ya."

"So, you can stop worrying. Your dream was just a nightmare." Shay slides a plate on the table for me with a breaded pork chop and potato mash. "You want a beer?"

"Sure," I say. "It wasn't a nightmare. Just a bad dream."

She ignores me. "How was the rest of your day?"

"Good. Same old. What about you?"

"You know my friend Doris, the one whose husband died up there at the plant?"

"Ya."

"Well, Doris had a fire last night at the house. She was frying chicken and the grease got away from her."

"She okay?"

"Sure, she's fine, but the house took off like a tinder box. Those old houses near the water plant are made of paper. I swear. I think that's the third fire down there in as many years."

Dinner is always like this with Shay, and I guess that is a good thing. We could sit quietly together, but I like this better. I don't have stories like she does. I don't think about life with stories. Shay seems to spend her whole days at work collecting stories to tell me. It's one of those things that makes her beautiful to me.

She moves from Doris to another drama about one of her customers. I'm thinking about Dice in a fire. I'm thinking of the thick skin of his jowls blistering and his mouth yelping like a pup as he tries to beat the flames off of him. I'm thinking about how I can stage such a thing and still be there to watch him go. I couldn't burn the trailer, and despite the sleazy clientele, I wouldn't burn down the strip club. There are lines I won't cross.

I don't sleep. I leave Shay with her gentle dreams and wander to the living room. There's a chair there that belonged to my mother before she sold the house. She's been up in Valeria for five years living with her sister. Besides the chair, there wasn't much else in the house that I wanted. The chair was hers. Everything else had the stain of my father on it. I sit in mom's chair and watch a pair of racoons rummage through the neighbour's garbage. I hear them chattering at each other in their rodent language.

I could go over there now, to Lucy's trailer. She sleeps deeply. I guess she needs some time to leave the world behind. I could pretend to be an intruder. Take something of value, the DVD player or the toaster oven or something. Dice would wake up. I know he would. I could hide in the bathroom and when he came looking, I could stab him in the belly and then slash his throat. His thick blood would run all over the floor. I could hold his mouth shut so he wouldn't scream. I'd go back there early in the morning, so that Lucy would just be waking up and I could protect her and Bird from seeing all of the mess and then call it in to the precinct like it was all a surprise to me.

When I wake up, I'm still sitting in mom's chair and the racoons are gone. There's trash all over the yard across and into the street and it's still dark outside. There are dull routines in life. I feel myself slipping into ruts and finding them comfortable. Eggs and tomato relish. A beer with dinner. Breaded pork chops. Shay snoring softly. Lucy looking sad and me worrying about her like I always have. Watching the irrelevant movements of raccoons negotiating their way around the human landscape. I can't stop thinking of Bird rocking back and worth confessing about Dice hitting his mother.

The house doesn't make enough noise at night. My whole life is noise, voices in my head, buzzing, whirring, rattling, clicking. I count on the noise to keep my thoughts down although that isn't working like it used to. Dice is big and loud in there, maybe the loudest of the ghosts rippling through every decent part of me, tearing down the fences and trampling the new grass. I want him dead. I want him dead more than I want anything else. I know killing him will break something in me. Hamlin's Creek isn't the crime capital of anywhere. A murder would be a big deal and I probably couldn't get away with it clean. Once, when I was just new on the job, I had to transfer a guy up the highway to the penitentiary. They assigned me a special car with a cage for a backseat and made sure I had another rookie partner for the ride just so we'd both feel lost and afraid. The rookie sat in the passenger seat and never took his hand off of his holster. I'm not sure how we made it safely there. I was sure that if the con in the cage even sneezed, the rookie would spring loose and kill everything in the car. I spent most of the time watching the con's eyes in the rear view, and the con spent most of the time watching his shoes. He had drowned his young son and strangled his wife. At the time, I would have said I didn't know what it was like to feel so black and desperate inside. Life teaches you all kinds of things I suppose.

I dab toast into the sour relish on my plate.

"What are you up to, Tom?"

"What do you mean?"

"You're restless. You're worrying all the time, talking about Lucy and Dice."

"I just worry about her, is all."

"You have to stop," Shay says. "She's a big girl, you know."

"Dice is bigger."

Shay looks down at her plate. She knits her hands together like she does when she's got worries of her own. I know she's disappointed in me.

"How's Doris?" I ask, trying to draw her out.

"Tom, that little girl has to live that life. You can't live it for her."

"I can help make her safe."

She looks at me for a long time while I finish breakfast.

"I made pie yesterday and forgot to serve it at dinner." Shay gets up and opens the fridge. "Do you want some now?"

"For breakfast?"

"What's wrong with that?" she asks.

"Well, pie is for dessert. You don't have pie with breakfast."

"And you don't live someone else's life for them either." Shay slams the fridge and walks off toward the bedroom. This is Dice's fault. I don't know what else to say to her. I have to do what I'm doing. I want to tell her that I have no other choice. Lucy is family. Without me, there'd be nobody to take care of her. I want to follow Shay, but I listen to the growl of the ceiling fan instead.

***

"Why do you come here like this, all angry and upset, Tommy? You don't have to come here all the time like this, you know?"

"I just stop by to make sure you're okay. Just looking out for you like a good brother should."

"Look out for what? For Dice?" Lucy is washing a couple of t-shirts in the sink. I don't ask her why. Dice isn't home at a time when he should be. The strip club closes at 4 a.m. and it's already 8 a.m.

"He's no good for you."

"You don't know what's good for me, Tommy. There are worse things I could be doing with my life."

"He hits you. He's not here for you when you need him."

She fumbles a water glass on the counter and it breaks. Blood oozes from a cut on her finger.

"I'll get you a bandage. I have a first aid kit in the car."

Lucy grabs a paper napkin and wraps it around her finger. "I'm fine. Don't worry."

"Put pressure on it."

"I know," she yells. "Tommy, I know this stuff. I know how to take care of myself."

"I'm just helping. I'm allowed to help you, aren't I?"

"I can't make you happy, Tommy. I can't make you happy and Dice happy and me happy all at the same time. It's too damn much. I've been trying to make men happy my whole life and it doesn't work like that. I have Bird to worry about and he's the only one I want to make happy. The rest of you are just in the way and, yes, you can be that way if you want, if it serves some good for you, but don't try to save me. You can't."

"But I've always been there for you. I've always been the one to protect you. I thought you…"

"You've never protected me, Tommy. Not like you might think."

"I kept Pa off of you, didn't I?"

She turns away, walks back down the trailer toward the bathroom and then turns. "You can't fight a dragon with a plastic sword."

It takes me a moment to understand her, as though she has spoken a foreign language. A sudden rushing sound fills my head so loudly that my other senses are paralyzed by it. I lose her. I lose the hum of the flies bouncing against the screen door, the television occupying Bird in his world. I imagine this is the hollow sound of death coming on. It is an impossible, stultifying, cold sound. I am gripped by it. Seduced by it, so that if it were the last thing I felt, the dark emptying of me like this, it would be okay. I could let everything go. I think I could. I think I'm that strong. Eventually, she comes back, the flies and the television too; she is halfway down the passageway of the trailer, the bedroom behind her. My legs are unsteady like the weight of me was somewhere else for a while. I find I can hardly even whisper.

"He got to you?"

She flutters her eyelids once for yes. "He got to me. He hit you, but he got to me."

From a faraway place, I hear Bird's echo: "He got to me."

I don't remember the rest of the day. I drive. I answer calls. I intervene in a domestic dispute. I pull over an old woman for DUI. I chase away some teenagers hassling kids in the park. The rushing sound never fades, not completely. The emptying continues. I watch mouths moves, angry drivers pushing their fists into their steering wheels. Rather than hear the sounds, I imagine the car horns bleating, tires squealing. I am caught up in the static. I am lying on her bedroom floor in a blue cape and tarnished yellow crown. The sword is beside me, ready to strike. In my sleep, the dragon spreads its vicious wings, swoops over me, and takes her.

I don't sleep again. Dangerously, I don't sleep. I imagine Dice dead. I imagine dragging him out of the trailer regardless of who is watching, plugging three rounds into his forehead and watching him bleed. Violent and unabashed ruthlessness. I imagine Lucy running to me, beating her angry fists against my chest, crying, but it doesn't matter. Dice is a dragon she does not see, or maybe she is just so used to the disaster of her life that she is blind to it.

You wouldn't figure it this way, but when I am not plotting his murder, I try to live a muted, simple life, the controlled madness of waking and all the rest of the polite luxury of civilized things. Somewhere in the background of all this pretending, the fan whirs over my head and rattles its teeth relentlessly.

Weeks pass before I think of going to see her, and that is only after Shay interrupts a football game on a Saturday afternoon.

"I have a feeling," she says. "Lucy's in trouble, Tom. I don't know how I know, but I know."

"She can take care of herself," I tell her. "Isn't that what you said?"

"This is different, Tom."

"Because it's your worry, not mine."

"We don't have to fight," she says. "If you don't go, then I will. You should go in your colours though."

"In my colours?"

"In your uniform," Shay says. "You'll have the respect of people around you."

"Only one person matters, right?" I mean Lucy, but after I think about it, Shay might have misunderstood who I meant, that I meant I wore the uniform to impress her.

"Just go, Tom. I know I said different. I know I let on that you should let her be. But I have a feeling."

She's already holding out the heavy police jacket she likes me to wear. It won't stop a bullet, but it makes me look larger than I am. I don't believe her about the uniform.

I don't want to see her. I've failed her. There is no shame in this for me, no regret, only the heavy weight of having misled myself, at having believed I was a hero for her. I feel it in my chest all of the time now, the coming of death, the rushing in my ears, the muffled way the world sounds to me, as though my head is tied inside a bag of water. The drive to the trailer park is strange. The trees are different, sticks in the wind. The sky faded ashen, not blue. I notice signs that I don't remember seeing before. I miss the turn, despite the large lit marker announcing Waymouth Mobile Home Community.

Lucy is screaming. Last night was cold and the doors and windows of the trailer are all sealed tight. Despite the cocoon she is in, I hear her cries as though she were beside me. The door is locked, so I kick at it until it opens. Bird is sitting at his regular perch. He doesn't even turn to acknowledge me. I hear a solid strike of flesh on flesh and a violent shudder shakes me as I remember the feeling of such a thing from the inside. I rush down the length of the trailer to the bedroom. Lucy is on the bed and Dice straddles her thin body, pinning her down, his fist raised for another hit. He turns when I burst in. There are no words. Lucy looks up, her eyes swollen from crying, one cheek blossomed rose red. He tries to stand on the bed and hits his head on the ceiling, an animal fierce with adrenaline, unaware of his cage. In a swift, wild motion, he rushes me and I trip backwards, spin, and find Bird hopping down the narrow passageway towards us. I manage to skirt him. I turn at the doorway and watch Dice blindly knock the boy over, a heavy foot comes down on the boy's leg, and the cracker snap of bones breaking fills the tiny space.

Bird doesn't cry out. He doesn't react when Dice's other calloused foot mashes the boy's tiny hand. The man's eyes are purple and blind with rage. I think he doesn't see me, but rather senses me as something threatening, not a person, not even a predator, just a thing, a thing that means to hurt him. There is one quick dance step as I dodge his attempt to grab me. I turn enough to open a space between me and the door. I smell him, thick with sweat and alcohol. In the moment Dice fills the small space, I shove his body with the full force of my slight frame.

Miraculously, he flies through the doorway and lands in the dirt and gravel outside. His body hits both sides of the frame and the trailer rocks like it has been struck by a train. I am still inside and expect him to come at me. I draw my night stick, prepared to strike him. All of my bravado, every fantasy about killing him rushes forward and bursts. Despite my anger, I am incapable. I am terrified of him, too frightened to do anything more than stand here with this thin stick slightly raised, not even sharp as a plastic sword. I know he will crush me, but I'm unable to muster anything more than this. I feel Lucy move behind me suddenly and then the explosion of a gunshot stings my ears, the heat so close I feel it on my face. She has stolen my service revolver. Dice stops. The first shot punctures his belly. The second shot hits his shoulder. He loses balance, but manages to right himself, grips one hand on the trailer to come at the both of us. The third shot hits him square in the chest. He falls backwards, still upright. His eyes cloud, his face suddenly grey. I imagine the sound he hears, the lightness he feels. The fourth shot misses him, but the fifth punctures his cheek and I see the spray of blood exit the back of his head before he falls. The next three shots, aimed at the space where he had been standing, miss him completely.

There is the white flare and there is the howling in my ears. There is neither joy, nor relief, nor pain. There is Lucy, standing at the tiny kitchenette, Bird on the floor behind her, injured, eyes wide, completely silent. My dry lips have nothing to say. She crouches; her dark eyes never stop watching me. She reaches back to touch Bird and he cries out with his small voice, "Okay, Mommy. Okay," but nothing is that way. She stands again slowly, and brings both hands to the pistol and trains it on me. It doesn't matter that it is empty.

"Get out," she says it and sighs heavily as though something awful in her is finally ready to escape. There is blood flowing freely from her split lip. I only notice now that her t-shirt is torn exposing one damaged breast. Dice has bitten her hard enough to leave marks and draw blood. "Get out," she says again. "And don't come back."

The world is such a loud, awful place of static sound. Before I reach the car, I hear the door behind me close, I hear the tiny clink of metal as the pieces of the broken latch come together and fail to meet properly. The only sound I hear after that is the insane ringing in my ears that does not stop.

There is no need for me to radio the precinct. The dog walkers have already gathered by my cruiser, cell phones out, thumbs busy. I think of leaving, but there is nowhere for me to go. Three other cruisers arrive before I have time to formulate a story, some way to explain this. One of the officers pulls me from the car and hands me a bright roll of yellow caution tape. I see his finger point, his mouth move, understand what he is saying, but never hear a word of it. I don't know where to start. I tie one end of the tape to the empty terracotta flower pot disguising the hitch of the mobile home. I walk slowly, drifting really, one hand extended to encourage the small crowd of gawkers back. I speed up, lost in the act of moving away from Lucy, the roll running out like a ribbon behind me. There is not enough of this tape to wrap her whole world. By the time I am sprinting out toward County Road 7, all of the caution tape is gone.

***

I am nursing a coffee in the kitchen. I haven't fixed the ceiling fan. Billy Joel on the radio, a song about fire. Bird is sitting on the floor in the living room, a cast on his little left leg and a large bandage on his right hand. I hear Shay talking to him.

"You okay, Bird?"
"Okay, Bird," he chirps as though nothing is wrong.

They arrested Lucy. One cop told me I wouldn't stop screaming as she was being handcuffed. I don't remember any of it. She is awaiting trial for manslaughter. Her lawyer will argue self-defence, but who knows. For the time being, I'm on mental health leave. I know it's a type of suspension and that I probably won't go back. Maybe I'll return to sales. Maybe real estate this time. I turn to watch Bird, who is playing with a little toy car that Shay bought him yesterday. He looks toward me and smiles. His face grimaces, then twists into a look of horror and pain. "Let her go," Bird shouts, mimicking the mess I'd made that day, a frantic expression of the terror I had spilled into his life. "I killed him. I did it. I did it. I killed him. Let her go. Let her go." And then he starts to howl, a sound so shrill and stark that it matches perfectly the unforgiving ringing in my ears.

In the Way never found a home in publication. I thought it should. I don't know if it's too shocking, too violent, or what the issues are with the story. There's a joke I heard as a kid that set this story in motion: How many boy scouts did it take to help an old lady across the street? Answer: Twelve. She didn't want to go.

This story is about will. Tom wants to save Lucy. She is on her own path where Tom is an intrusion. No matter his good intentions and his perception of Lucy's life, she is making it happen. She and Bird might have had an ordinary sort of life had it not been for Tom's intervention. For a long time, I believed that everyone aspired for some degree of greatness or success. I've come to understand that some people just want to be ordinary. In this story, Tom ends up the villain rather than the hero, in part because he wants something for his sister that she doesn't want. Sometimes you just leave "well-enough" alone. As difficult as that is.

In the din of the seething, protesting waves, I cannot describe the ocean's language with words. The tumult of it horrifies. You will not hear me. My mouth is full of water.

Sky and then sea, and then George laughing, hollering some vulgar, bastard language in a guttural drunken drawl, he swings my thin body high over his head like a kite, holds me there exposed to the cool Northwest wind, torturing, waiting for the right break in the surf.

"Stop squirming, you little sissy," he screams. "Have some damned fun." George squeezes my leg and arm tight enough to bruise, but I am otherwise so paralysed that I do not feel his iron hands crushing me. He pushes out further into the bay, foam rising to cut me with its chill, the stony shore of Puget Sound echoes back my desperate cries, shriller than killdeers or seagulls. Finally, mercilessly, he launches me, not sailing, gently, safely lobbed, but viciously thrown, a thrall to the cold and terrifying sea. I am scraped against the rough seabed, one swell and then another rolls me like an empty shell. George finds me by thrusting his fist into the brine and cracking me in the jaw. I am probably unconscious when he draws me out, rank, salty mucous and sea water flowing freely from my nostrils. I hear only the roar in my ear, not loud, but painful. I feel him shaking me. I try to will my heart to stop, my throbbing thoughts to evaporate. I gasp at the same moment that he laughs, lifts me again, and thrusts me back out into the horror. This is George: Never tender. Never sober.

George beat my mother to death without laying a hand on her. He just wore her out with his largeness, his arrogance, his jabs, his taunts. He moved through the house like a deranged locomotive who thought himself better than tracks. She holds me tightly, spooning me in her bed, weeping silently, whispering to me. The smell of her is so sour, so strong, that I stop up my ears and do not listen to her as she fades away. In the middle of the night, when I am dragged from her arms, groggy, barely in the world, I do not know that she has left it.

***

At the psychologist's office, the walls in the waiting room are not panelled with oak or maple. They are plain and paper white. The artwork mounted in brushed aluminum frames is unpretentious. Stock images, gentle colours, no pastels and no shocking blues or blacks. Nothing as bold as Rothko or Kahlo, or God forbid, Van Gogh. Perhaps the work is well-placed, thoughtfully selected to soothe without metaphysical challenge. You would not mistake this for anywhere interesting.

The stiff metal chairs in the waiting room ignore me. I choose to stand, however awkwardly: I struggle for a place to rest my hands, for a comfortable posture. I settle for holding my arms still, dangling rather than swimming in my pockets or floating through a magazine. Suddenly, my discomfort is interrupted by a soft-voiced woman who invites me through a swinging door. "Doctor Racz-Müller is ready for you." She leads me down a wide passageway lined with plastic plants. First, a stockroom. Then, a coffee room. A room with several more chairs and a kidney-shaped table. Another room behind a door. Mumbles and whispers. At the end, a small room with a desk, a chair, a narrow leather sofa, a cosy bookcase, and by the window, a table with a Ficus plant, this one real.

Doctor Racz-Müller's eyes consider me thoughtfully over a grocery-store pair of reading glasses. He bows his head and scribbles something in his notes. I have landed here, adult, not plain like the white walls, nor vague or abstract like the art. I have arrived at the invitation of a benevolent employer who would rather me healed than absent another day from my job.
"You still take care of him."
"Who?"

"George, your father," the doctor says. "You take care of him."

"Just George." Behind the doctor, the window is wide, the sky beyond is blue, filled with wisps of cloud. "Don't call him my father. He is not that."

"You take care of George."

"*Care* is too intimate," I say, boring myself with semantics. "I tend to his needs."

"You are a good person."

I look into my hands and feel the unfortunate cliché of the moment. I smile the terrible wan grin that accompanies the story that cannot be told. The smile is not a mask, not forced, nothing as conscious as that. This version of *smile* comes at the extreme opposite of joy where madness begins to pull open the psyche and cry all over it.

"You're smiling," he says.

Anything I can tell him about the smile will only deepen the cliché, make what I feel either moot or absurd. Of course, on many levels, I know the answer is nothing like this, that what I might say could not be unwound as easily as the artwork in the waiting room. I hate it, tending to George. I hurt in ways that do not have words. I tend to George. I do what I have to do. He is a cramp that twists every time I try to catch my breath.

***

The tourists, most of them Canadians, hover by the pool, waiting. I know their story. They hoped to lose a few pounds before boarding their flights to Florida, or climbing into their RVs or Buicks for the drive here. Procrastination and bad habits always get in the way. So, here they are at the Bluegrass Inn, only a few yards from the Atlantic Ocean, hoping I can coach some weight off before they shuffle down the beige sand. The hotel's name has nothing to do with Appalachian music. Rather, the Northerners who built the place tore out all the native grass that reminded them of kissing grandpa's stubbly face, and replaced the lawn with soft artificial turf. I would have appreciated cork or rubber or even tile, but the nylon seems to suit the tourists. I begin stretching, one arm and then the other. The tourists watch and follow my lead. Twenty or thirty minutes of dancercise, yoga, or gentle cardio. The workout doesn't do much for their physique, but when I am done with them they are likely limber enough for the water. By afternoon, they will feel equally ready for a greasy dinner and be back on the faux lawn in the morning, guilty, hungover, and hungry for more of what I do.

***

"You came an awfully long distance to be a fitness trainer," the doctor says.

I decide not to argue about the job title. "I didn't feel like staying in Washington."

"You're as far away as you can get."

He won't ask a question. He doesn't have a direction. He coughs. He hums. He writes in the little notebook on his desk. He waits for a confession I do not have, for an admission from me that will not form. It is too early to trust him.

"I shouldn't have come." I say this, but in the recitation, I recognize that this too is clichéd, that I am trapped in this paradigm. I stand, and yet cannot leave. My hands flounder with no place to rest. I do not understand what it means to heal, what it would mean to be any different than what I am. Doctor Racz-Müller doesn't protest, and this too is clichéd. *Let the patient lead where he may.* I know this script, not because I am trained in such things, rather, it just seems obvious. Why should the doctor assault me with questions? He knows I will not leave. He knows I am bound here. I might lose the job I have if nothing in me changes.

***

The first time I lift a brick, it is to pass it up a ladder to George. The Northwest rain has found a flaw in the roof and he is up there laying a tarp to keep the water from ruining the floor since it has already stained the ceiling. The brick is cold and rough in my small, delicate hand. It hurts at the elbow to lift, and I feel the tightening in my shoulder and bicep as I climb to him with the weight above my head. I am so small, but still managing the weight. I imagine myself an ancient warrior. I imagine myself fierce. Just as I am ready to call out to the tribe, George looks down at me, catches the look on my face and laughs. I know not to react. He will only poison his assault with words. After only a dozen bricks, George climbs down, disappears inside where I expect he will finish whatever bottle he is involved with at the moment. I carry another brick. The pain is big in my little muscles. I climb. I set the thing on the edge of the roof. I climb down. I let the fierceness in my face return, careful to listen for his footfalls on the patio. I climb again; remove the brick with the other arm. I do this until I am shaking, in a dizzy rush, nearly unable to grip the aluminum rungs of the ladder. In pain, I find power. In pain, the adrenaline fills me with strength. Pain empties all of George out of me, makes him small against my warrior self. But I am only salt. When I finish, stow the ladder away, and wander back inside, all of that courage dissolves.

Later, when my body matures, the muscles bulge in my arms, across my chest. I stand at the mirror and flex. The pain has made me beautiful, thin, hard, corded with rippled flesh. I study myself standing sideways, over my shoulder. The part that matters is that I know George has also noticed and that he hasn't raised a hand to me for some time. I expect he worries that I might defend myself. The reflection in the mirror is a lie. He is large, but I am stronger. He might not be able to lift me, but he could still beat me down.

***

There is a cup of coffee on the doctor's desk that is probably cold because he hasn't touched it since I sat down. I can smell the cloying sweetness of it. Two creams and too much sugar. There are two frames on the desk facing away from me: A wife? Partner? A pet? Children? Perhaps more of the art from the waiting room, images purchased with the frames. He will not let me read him and I wonder why he is behind the desk and not out here with me, sitting in the other chair, unprotected, unmasked. He has good hair and fair skin. He isn't very old, but older than I am. Maybe forty. I watch his mouth move when he talks.

"Why are you in Florida?" I ask him, testing to see if he will become defensive, defer to bland platitudes about the weather and redirect right back to me. I wonder if he is cordial or warm, genuine, sincere.

"I was born here."

"You didn't long to go somewhere else?" I ask.

"I travel, but this is home for me, as I expect it is home for you."

"It's not my home. It's just a place." I stop and see right away what he has done.

"It's a place to leave George," he says.

"George is luggage. He is a box that belongs in the carport for eventual discard."

"It surprises me that you brought him such a long way when you might have left him in Seattle."

"Taking care of George happens. That's all. He is old and sick. I just take care of him. It's a thing I do and then I don't think about it. I don't think about opening a can of tuna for myself, or pouring cereal into a bowl. It is just part of the ritual."

As he should, Doctor Racz-Müller scribbles into his little book. I think he is single. The frames on the desk might be empty.

***

"Get me the piss jar, Travis," George groans. Despite his age, his disease, he still barks like a younger, bigger dog.

"No," I say softly and turn CNN a little louder and listen to reports about the storm season along the Atlantic Coast. I don't go in the water. I don't go near the water. George has given me all I need of water. I watch the tides warily from the hotel lawn, and ignore the ocean the rest of the time. The Atlantic is no better than the Pacific.

"I'll piss myself," George whines.

"You're not invalid. Get up and go find the toilet."

"You're just like your mother," he says softly. "A prissy little sissy-boy."

"I'm going out."

I don't know why I am compelled by him. I drop the remote, walk to the bedroom to retrieve his urine bottle, and lay it on his lap. Instead of setting back to the news, I walk through the kitchen to the back of the house where a small screened veranda keeps my exercise equipment. Today, I choose the elliptical. After forty minutes, I stop for a glass of water. Pouring the drink reminds me of salty brine choking my tiny throat and running out my nose. It is dark outside. Forty more on the treadmill and then I am empty. I have a headache. I am thirsty again, but sleep will be better than the panic of pouring another drink. I have heard him calling me. He has filled his bottle and then likely wet himself. There is always alcohol nearby to distract him so cleaning him up can wait until morning.

In the dream, I stand at the water's edge, the frigid stink of Puget Sound; the wash threatens to swallow my feet in ice. Above my head, struggling, suffocating, George screams a hoarse, wild anthem of terror. I wake up soaked in sweat. It is still dark outside. I find George on the couch and the smell of him suggests he has done more than wet himself. He barely stirs as I carry him to the bathroom and place him in the empty tub. He is diapered like an infant, but I refuse to find anything sad or tragic about him. He is aging, but he is sturdy, rugged. He survived a lightning strike in Oregon when he was working the lumber camps. The Lichtenberg patterns interlace his leg, his neck, his shoulder. Fractal equations desperate to be solved, the tender pink scars swell when he drinks, as some ancient language crying out to be deciphered. I think I was an infant when it happened. I imagine him waking in the hospital (or maybe prone on the denuded hill where he was hit) and not feeling lucky, not feeling grateful that his life is spared. Rather, I know George probably laughs from deep in the middle of his chest, a satisfied feeling that he has become a king, or worse, a god. He has become who he becomes and nothing more. I leave him unconscious, pathetic, in the empty tub. In the morning, he can wash himself.

***

The third visit to Doctor Racz-Müller begins with a jarring challenge. "You should run on the beach." He extends a hand which I think he intends for me to shake before it is clear that he is only directing me to sit.

"You mean down by the water?"

"Exactly, that," he says calmly. "It's a beautiful run. I've done it myself. The sand and air are wonderful." I try to imagine him in running shorts or spandex. He is still standing by his desk and I study his trousers and try to make out the shape of his legs beneath.

"I don't go near water. I've told you that."

"Stay on the wet sand," he says, as he sits behind the desk again. "It's softer than the sidewalk, but still firm."

"I don't go near water."

"You should." He writes something down. "I mean, you need to, Travis." He says my name often, usually to punctuate something he wants me to notice. I know that it is a trick, and yet, it is a thrill to hear him personalize me.

"If I run on the beach, will I be healed?" I ask. "Is that what you're telling me, Doctor? If I rub mud in my eyes, I'll have second sight?" I realize it sounds sarcastic, but I can't take it back. There is nothing I can add to soften the question.

"You can try that, I suppose," he says, unmoved. "You won't ever walk on water, if that's what you want from me."

"Why should I do what you ask then? If you don't give me miracles, then what's the use? It's miracles that I need."

"You don't have to do anything I ask," he says, but then reads the frustration on my face. "I should give you a straight answer – No, a helpful answer." He pauses, considers me for a moment, but then his eyes drift, first to the books, then he turns in his chair to look out the window and then back again to me. I think I frustrate him, maybe even overwhelm his training. As a client, I am an aberration. "You'll make your own miracles, Travis." He pauses and writes again, separates from me. I can tell from his posture that I have upset him. He is writing about his inability to provide magic for me, a breakthrough moment for one or both of us. I want to ask him about the frames on his desk. The timing is wrong.

***

He hits me. It is regular, not predictable. I never see him hit Mom, though George has a temper that rattles the dishes. One stormy night, I stand by the stairs and study him in the kitchen rubbing his neck with one hand, the other grips the back of Mom's chair. She looks nervous, but tries not to. She steeps a teabag in and out of a china cup. He massages his own neck, but what I think is that he is warming up his hand for a slap, or stopping himself from something worse. He asks Mom something I don't hear. She doesn't understand or doesn't answer. His voice bawls so loudly that I wonder if the neighbours might fly over to see what the matter is. When he finally explodes, his hand slams so hard against the table that her cup bursts and hot tea splashes all over Mom. I watch her. She doesn't flinch. In that moment, I believe she is a china cup just a crack away from breaking.

***

Before the fourth visit with the doctor – and I must go back – I determine to run, not only outside, but also on the beach as he has suggested. The sidewalks and roads are uneven, dirty, cracked, the surfaces harder than the treadmill and I have to concentrate with each step so as not to twist an ankle or break a leg. The sun is strong and relentless. By the time I cover the ten miles between the house and the Bluegrass Inn, I am already tired. I hear the ocean before I see it. I smell the acrid, salty, air that hovers near the shore. My senses conspire against my will and I have to run another five miles down the highway to the gates of Palmetto Gardens Park and then back again before I can courage my way down the beach to the shoreline. First there is the hot, dry, wretched sand to contend with, slow and slippery, nearly impossible to move through. I watch shore birds skitter back and forth with the scalloped ebb of the ocean. The beach is deserted but for me and the birds. I run a mile, keeping to the wet parts where the compacted sand is smooth and even, dodging and jumping over the sea foam, dead jellyfish, and drifts of rotting seaweed. The time is wrong and the tide is crawling, foreshortening my path with every new wave. I can hardly breathe for fear of being swept in. After a mile, I am back on the dry beach dragging and tripping as I run. Another few hundred yards back on the wet hard pack, then abandon the effort, race for the stairs behind a row of white condominiums and I am done. I have met the challenge and when the doctor asks – he won't ask, he will say, *tell me about your run* – I do not have to avoid a response or lie. I will recite the catechism – I have run the beach – and it will be the truth. It was a failure, but he will not ask. The race back to the house is executed at sprinter's pace, penance for not sustaining the beach for longer. I finish on the elliptical before collapsing into the armchair to listen to George moan. A marathon to discover nothing has changed.

In the past month, George has emptied a large bottle of drugstore pain killers, complaining of an ache in his belly. When he bleeds in his urine, I force him to the hospital.

***

"They found cancer," I tell Doctor Racz-Müller who leans toward me, his fingers knitted across the desk. "They can't operate on him. Already, he is working with one kidney, his liver is more tumour than healthy organ, and they believe his pancreas is also tainted."
"If you throw him in the ocean now, it will be an act of mercy."
"I shouldn't have told you about my dreams."
"You love him," Doctor Racz-Müller says. "I don't understand why."
"I don't love him."
"But you can't kill him."
"I won't kill him. That's absurd."
"You don't hate him."

I question what I have said, everything I have told the doctor. I do not love George, cannot love him. I have carried him all the way from Seattle, tolerated him, fed him, sheltered him, even nursed his diseases. I don't know why, I just do what I do. The doctor is right, I do not hate George. But it cannot be love. Perhaps another version of love. Revenge love. Addictive love. Masochism. Adulation. The love of kings. Or fear, the love of God.

"No." I say it again so that Doctor Racz-Müller can be sure about what I have determined. "I do not love him."

Oddly, the doctor moves from behind the desk and leaves his notepad. He sits, not in the empty armchair, but beside me on this narrow leather sofa, leans back comfortably, stretches, sighs, scratches his head, looks out the window for a long time, then returns to me, rests his warm hand on mine. "What is it then, Travis? What is it you feel for him?"

After so many weeks in this office, it is the first question, and I hate it. I do not want the question. I do not want to hear another thing he says to me. He doesn't know me. He doesn't know anything. I can neither breathe nor catch my breath. I am drowning in the shallows off the rocky coast of Puget sound and the doctor stands beside George, both of them laughing.

"You know, Travis," he says, arrogantly. I see him now, pompous, self-absorbed, controlling. "You don't have to *be* him. You don't have to like him, or even care for him. You've heard that before, I bet. It means that you're safe moving out from under the tremendous, punishing weight of the man. That would be okay. He can't hurt you. In fact, he will die more peacefully, and you will be freer to let him go."

I pull my hand out from under his, stand and step away from where he sits looking up at me. "I have told you so many things and still you don't know anything about me." I move toward the door, certain that I must leave and never come back. There is no healing here for me. "And certainly, no miracles," I say aloud and only later wonder why I have done so.

For a time, I thought we'd connected the doctor and me. He often smiled when I felt he might smile, when I wanted to know that he understood my feelings. I was wrong though. He is a fraud. He is no better than a psychic or fortune teller, a charlatan, a joke. His art is cheap. I was supposed to strike into a breakthrough moment, some clarity of mind or peace of conscience. I leave quickly, filled with vile feelings over his charade, the facade, the counterfeit he has put me through.

On the way out, I pass the empty coffee room, the plastic plants, the small empty alcove where the secretary usually sits. The murmurs, the mumbles, the secretive whispers. All of it is worse than plain. It is cheap. The carpeting is cheap. The furniture is cheap. In the vacant waiting room, I stop to straighten one of the abstract prints on the wall. I am neither in the lines nor in the spaces. I am not colour and I am not light. I am shadows, wisps of clouds against a pale sky. I am not George. I am nothing at all. A shell eroding on the ocean floor. I am nowhere, nobody. I wait a moment to see if the doctor will come after me. When he doesn't, I leave.

At home, George is moaning, suffering really, and I have nothing left to give him. He smells sweaty, septic, old, used up.
"Where have you been?" he barks. "I needed you."
"You're dying."
"Not fast enough."
"One day, you're going to call for me and I won't be here."
"You have nowhere to go, you little puke. Don't pretend you do."
"I'm not your slave anymore."
"You're me," he growls. "I made you. When I am gone, there will be you. That makes me immortal, doesn't it?"

I look over at him, his face twisted with anger, his body beaten by his own flawed psyche. I am not him. I am sculpted, fit, handsome. I am not a god, not a king. I am only. I remember having been weak enough that he could hurt me.

"I am not you," I try. "I am not you. You are nothing, and I am something."

"What are you? You're a dance instructor or something, aren't you? What are you? You're nothing. I moved logs bigger than you when I was twice your age."

"That isn't true. You stopped logging before I —" There is something in him that wants to keep clawing at me, a carrion eater, an unmaker, a parasite. There is nothing left in me for him, but George goes on trying to take.

"I'm going running."

"What about my meds? I need my meds."

"I told you, call all you'd like. I'm not here for you."

"Travis!" I hear him calling from the back door. "Travis!" I still hear him as I cross the yard. By the time I am around the corner, I only hear him in nagging memory. I can manage that.

This time I run directly to the beach, no distractions, no easing in to this. It is late, nearly dark. The wind is strong, and I can feel the cold of an autumn storm rolling in. The clouds over the ocean hang overhead, angry and gloomy, broiling with certain fury. I sprint along the wet shore, still wary of the sliding foam gliding rhythmically up and back into the sea. I am not George. I am not lover or loved. I can do without the doctor. I don't need his petty conversation, his lack of interest, his guarded, oblique dialogue. I can do all of this alone. When George dies, there will be no mourning in me. I can let him die; for that alone, the doctor is right — I will be free of him.

With the corner of my eye I catch something that I first mistake as a dolphin struggling over a wave. I think of the many times I dreamed or imagined carrying George here to throw him in or simply seat him down on the beach to wait for high tide. None of those images are anything like this. There is someone out there, a real person, arms fighting for the surface, mouth agape, coughing, choking. I am stopped, watching him, the drowning man. I can't breathe. I can't help him.

I left Puget Sound to escape my mother's ghost. She would come to me every night, crawl into bed, wrap her cold dead arms around my belly, caress me, whisper lies, how beautiful, how strong, how noble I was. She did not follow me to Florida except for the occasional possession by one of the Snowbirds: her hair, her mouth, or her peculiar gait. On the plastic lawn one day, a woman approaches me, gazes through mother's soft blue eyes; she hugs me as I stiffen and tells me what a beautiful coach I am. If I'd left

George in Washington State, he would have called me back to all of that horror and I would have lost my mind.

An arm flails desperately out in the surf.
"I can't help you!"

Another wave covers the man in the surfing shirt. He struggles and then goes under again.

"I can't help you!" I scream, and have to skitter up the beach to avoid the angry tide. Behind me, the sun dips below the white condominiums. I turn and yell for help, but the beach is lost in shadow. The renters have likely moved inland in advance of the storm. The sky is fire red, cloud-to-cloud lighting stitches the twilight, thunder pounds without pause.

The water suddenly grabs my feet and a swift wave wraps around my legs and knocks me over. I scramble like an animal, screaming, yelping: "Help," I cry. "Help." The man has gone under, the clock in my head winds down and the bells ring wildly. The swimmer is down there. I know where he is, rolling beneath the waves. I have been there before, water running in and out of my mouth without obstruction.

"I can't help you," I scream again and lift myself to see if the swimmer will appear.

The waves reach for me again. Without thought, I am howling now, charging into the spray, every muscle in my legs cramp at the same time, rippling with the fear that is in me. I walk in dream-speed, move without moving, advance without advancing, the goal, the destination draws further and further from me, then suddenly there is something heavy at my feet. I punch down through the agonizing wash and find an arm, drag the body to the surface, and rush for shore. He is lifeless, and I wonder if there is enough left in me to share with him. Again, the target evades. The sea wants to steal us both. My body aches from the cold Atlantic, my heart staccatos inside my chest barely able to sustain the effort it takes to be here.

There are people on the beach, a couple, and then three others, chasing down the sand from the white condominiums. One of them holds a cell phone above her head trying to tell me something. Suddenly, I feel the wet hair on my neck peel away from my skin and stand on end. I am encompassed in the effervescent static that precedes the flash. There is a brilliant explosion behind me, sound and light at the same time, the entire beach glows white. For a moment, there is neither sea nor air, only the deep blue of night. There are no sounds, only the erratic rhythm in my chest. Then someone is pulling us, dragging both of us up to the shore. My legs fail and though I let *myself* go, I cling tightly to the drowned man.

Love of Kings hasn't been published before. Much of my writing involves characters trying very hard to come out from under a force or circumstance which is overwhelming. The myth of Sisyphus is a strong reference for me. Little dog against the big dog.

I'm not sure if Travis manages to save himself, or whether, in the end, he drags a corpse to shore. He might not be dragging a literal corpse. He might have had a breakdown. It might be himself he is dragging through the fray. The woman on the shore with her cellphone in the air, worried as she is, may be imploring him to save himself from the storm. What she doesn't know is that the storm he lives in easily eclipses the pending hurricane. As tight as Travis feels inside, his story has a lot of loose ends. The *Georges* in our lives have a tendency to leave us frayed/afraid and even broken.

"And as to you Life I reckon you are the leavings of many deaths"
~ *Walt Whitman, <u>Song of Myself</u>*

this is a road you know

a space and then a line

a space and then a line

The one wiper makes a grating sound as it rakes across the windshield. The other wiper follows, but the car is out of washer fluid, so most of what you see is a smear.

a space and then a line

Daddy stops the car on a hill and drags you out of your sleep so that you can see the aurora, though you can't quite make it out, because you are so cold, but as soon as you crawl back into the car and he starts driving again you look out the back window and the sky is on fire with green and blue light. It is the most fantastic moment of your young life, and you hug at Daddy's neck from the backseat with tears in your eyes.

a space and then a line

There are tears without a thought to justify. The newspaper on the seat next to you shifts as you round a corner on the highway, and you move your hand over to slide it back into place, careful not to touch Trevor's picture on the front page.

You remember a dream you had a few nights ago: you forget the kids at a campground play area – Jeremy in the little swing with the safety bar pulled down so that he cannot wiggle out, and Marnie at the picnic table draws on the back of a Chinese restaurant placemat with the only three crayons you can find for her.

a space and then a line

a space and then a line

On this road, Zack Turner decides to get into his little Isuzu truck after drinking three beers too many. His error might not be a problem, since he only lives down in the shallows. Halfway home, a big buck wanders across the yellow line, and the poor creature slides neatly up the hood through the windshield and takes most of Zack's head off. The pair bleeds to death flailing around in a frantic survival dance.

You have an English degree that you pay for by working in a call center, activating cell phones. You might summarize your education in a few lines of verse. The summary might look like:

\a red wheelbarrow beside the white chickens\
\two roads diverged in a yellow wood\
\And I will love you still, my Dear\
\Till all the seas go dry\
      \I am in the lake\
      \in the center\
      \And not waving but drowning\

You might add how they dragged you from under the house to pick the worms off of you like sticky pearls, but by now you would be paraphrasing. If you were to go much further, the whole of it would delineate\devolve into conjecture, detritus, flotsam, hyperbole. That is the right word:

\hyperbole\   ~ n. an exaggeration too heavily borne

After the call center, there is the hospital laundry where you fill your senses
with more wretched odours than one mind ought to manage. Trevor is an
orderly who begins to bring meaning to your life. Then he is an author, but he
cannot write. And then he is a pilot who is afraid of heights. So, he sinks all of
his

\your\

money into the car you are driving. You pay for the car with a broken arm
and a shattered orbital bone, and now you have to wear special corrective
lenses to keep everything from blurring up – and you think how this is a
metaphor. Somewhere between the hospital laundry, Trevor, the leaving him,
there are children, but they are not yours.

In the newspaper, after Trevor's picture, the first line is peculiar, very nearly
obscure:

"Women who kill their children..."

a space and then a line

You are driving and cannot read at the same time. The cell phone under the
newspaper vibrates. You ignore it. They are not even your children

\Trevor\   ~ n. a monumental mistake in judgment

Trevor points out their mother at the mall food court. She looks too stoned
to notice you and too thin, too papery, to walk over to the children. She
would probably not recognize them. You wonder if she would recognize
herself. You wonder if Trevor did this to her, or whether she did it to herself.
This is before he breaks your arm. You glance in the rear-view mirror and
note that your face has changed since the surgery. You have trouble
remembering what you used to look like. Trevor is a mess. But the children,
who somehow ended up with you, are unbearable. Jeremy is too young to
speak, and because of the steady infusion of gin through the umbilical there is
some question about what, if anything, he might be able to say. Marnie, unless
heavily medicated, will not stop talking. She likes to recite things. As adamant
as Ferlinghetti, as dialectic as Whitman.

a space and then a line

a space and then a line

Right now, you are driving the beige Dodge Charger that Trevor bought instead of paying his student loans. One wiper grates across the passenger side and leaves a smear. The other wiper is no better, but that has more to do with the precipitation, which is neither snow nor rain but some sticky wet muck that blurs the road enough to remind you of the feeling you have almost all of the time with Trevor. Well, not at first, because at first it is never like that. At first, it is like a red, red rose. At first, it is all infatuation and flutter. Only afterwards is it a blurred intensity that falls somewhere between hatred and addiction. An itch you cannot scratch. A cliché. But, the precipitation is a metaphor. No, the precipitation is pathetic fallacy. A portent of things to come. And even though it is April, there might still be snow.

You decide that Trevor should be blamed for so much of what is going on. But that would be superficial, and there is more to it than that. It begins with the red wheelbarrow and the little cottage where you first lived. This is where you are driving to, because sometimes to go the right way, it is necessary to go back to the beginning. And this is the road, the one Daddy used to drive, where the hills go up and down and up and down like a camel's back, and where Mommy makes him stop the car one night and wake you up and pull you out of your fog to behold the northern lights. And this is a story Mommy tells you later, not something you can actually remember. But afterwards, every time you are on this road you think about the wavering green and blue of the aurora and wish that you remembered for real, not simply as an addendum tacked on to your memory. Something Mommy gave you. And because you were there, you have a sense that perhaps you should feel guilty for not remembering: like they both did so much for you, and why, oh why, do you insist on messing it up all of the time by forgetting all of the good things? After all, Mommy tells you, and repeats it, there were many many good things. Iterations of good things. Mommy gave you the logic to find the good things and nothing but. A simple function, really.

a space and then a line

a space and then a line

It is here on this road, two winters ago, that a snowstorm traps thirty-four cars. The army is called upon to rescue stranded drivers. The actual count is thirty-five, but one car leaves the road and is not discovered until spring. You wonder what it must have been like for the driver, the wind and snow slowly cocooning her, drifting her into the landscape. You think about the simple function of volition, a moment when she lets it happen rather than fighting her way to the road for help. Perhaps she decides that sitting in the car is better than anything. You are awed at what it must have been like waiting for the cold to rid her of all the heavy burdens of life. In the newspaper, you read that she is older, retired, living alone, not missed by anyone but a cat, who also perishes while waiting for her return. Four months before anyone notices. A simple function of volition, perhaps a moment filled with deep euphoria as she realizes that soon she will be clothed in white, a phoenix, a butterfly, a metaphor for *angel* – something better than human.

You have a vision of yourself with the children, the ones who belong to Trevor. The camping is tense, but the children enjoy marshmallows and hot chocolate. In the morning, you pack the car to leave, and in the rear-view, Marnie is at the picnic table with the three crayons that have not melted in the sun the day before, and Jeremy is in the swing with the safety bar slid right down the chain to keep him there, and you feel compelled to leave them and cannot stop the car to

a space and then a line

a space and then a line

Life is like a road that way. A simile poorly placed. The tires hum, all tires hum, and it doesn't matter if they are cheap or fancy: volition chooses whether you will hum along or sing a different song.

a space and then a line

Ahead on the road is a sign you recognize, and you know it without having to read it. You cannot actually remember ever reading it. A sign you have noted since before you had words. The sign contains a hieroglyph that designates home. It is a demarcation. And you have never called it Avery Road or *the old concession road* as locals call it. For you, it is *the cottage road,* and this is the exit that takes you there.

\there\ ~ adv. referent for the geography where the uncle man touches you for the first time, and ever after without letting go

The cottage road winds away from the beach, back up into the trees, where there are other cottages before it winds around to the other side of the lake. The uncle man lives back there, but you have never been to his house. He always comes to yours, chats with Mommy and Daddy, eats at the table, helps with the dishes. And while Mommy and Daddy go out to the movies, the uncle man walks you into the yard and sits you in the long grass and does the things he has to do while you listen to the redwing-blackbirds mew and caw in the cattails. He is not really a relation, but it doesn't matter, really.

a space and then a line

The cottage road delineates down to the beach, but it also slopes up to a rocky outcropping where there is room for a dozen cars to park before the ledge falls sharply down to the lake. When you are small, you watch the teenagers park their cars up there and jump from the rocks to the water. You ask Mommy if you are allowed up there, but she tells you *no*. And you are twelve the first time you jump from the rocks, and Mommy is nowhere around. The driver is eighteen, the brother of a friend. Just being here is great and you are filled with euphoria. But the feeling passes when the rest of the teenagers leave or walk home, and you are a little afraid, but he sits you up on the hood and calls you pretty, brushes your hair back with sandy fingers, touches your cheek, and it is the last time you feel this way. You watch the sky blaze red and purple.

a space and then a line

And you check in the rear-view, but you cannot see the children, and you would like to say that it is tears obstructing your vision, but it is something rather more indeterminate. You see the scar on your face that still blisters red from where surgeons rebuilt the bone. There is still something missing along the cheek, across the thin lips, and the sad eyes. You think that that thing has been absent for a very much longer time.

a space and then a line

The sour weather will not let up, and the sky will not clear. The only thing holding you on the rocky outcrop is the parking brake, and it will take just a small function of volition to

a space and then a line

Torsion fracture. You say it in your mind and enjoy the cacophony. Trevor wrenches your arm behind your back and palms the back of your head; the wall comes rushing toward you, and for a moment you have time to wonder if you will hit the wall frame – the stud – or the soft drywall space in between, whether you will stop here in the kitchen or break right through to where Marnie and Jeremy are parked in front of the television, oblivious.

a space and then a line

In the long grass, you wonder what a trash it would be if each cattail ended at a cat waiting to pounce, every tiny bird marked with a little red target on each wing. The uncle man, with his eyes red from crying, he would not be safe from the cats and their claws. With each swish of the tail, each swish of his tail, you wish for cats and claws, scabbards and swords. You stare more deeply into the grass and try to forget each swish of the tail. Two words for victim:

\quarry\　　　　　v. to dig, related to stone
n. prey (homophone for supplications)

\supplication\ makes you think of sublimation – something else entirely.

a space and then a line

Beside you on the passenger seat is a newspaper. You read about Trevor; the story is appalling. There are loose sheets of paper here too, printed from the internet, and a copy of the story you sent to the uncle man's daughter – you remember her, older than you, one of the teenagers; you were never friends

her cold empty eyes

a space and then a line

you check the rear-view but can't find your eyes in the blur

The cell phone rings again and when you glance down, Trevor grins up at you from the newspaper, and for a moment you believe he is calling you. He is only a picture, a mosaic of grey dots in the newspaper, so you ignore the call again.

Something stirs behind you, and you think that it cannot be so, that the cherry-flavoured cough syrup has worn off so easily. You were so certain they would both sleep through.

The tall grass: a cunning place to hide. You can pretend to be innocuous, or even beautiful, the darker reality stolen by the blaze of blue and green light. The uncle man speaks softly as though telling secrets, but none of his words exist in memory; the sound of his voice is a hieroglyph signifying something else entirely.

Here is the place on the road where Trevor laughs at you, undoes his seatbelt, and steps out of the car while it is still moving. You have to slide over to the driver's side and stomp on the brake. You turn the car around, rush back, screaming, panicked, certain he has died. He laughs at you again, punches you in the head to force you back over to the passenger seat.

a space and then a line

a space and then a line

There is a necessary logic to justify your presence here. The words will not equate properly and you think you may have made a syntax error.

\Sin\tax\   ~ n. the price you pay for being wrong

You think that you have been wrong for a long time. You were born wrong, raised wrong, and all of the rest. The words are not enough.

\tax\   ~ n. measured in numbers, percentages

Language leaves for something more symbolic. Through the blur you can only make sense in small dialectic bursts. You might summarize thus:

\let x stand for *Trevor*\
\and y is the exponent signifying *uncle man*\
\consider x to the power of y\
\the multiplicand N can stand for anyone who pounded you against the hood of a car and treated every part of you below and above your crotch as insignificant\
\therefore, Nx^y\

You must also add the two in the backseat, the two who are not your issue, the two who are strapped in safe as produce

\issue\   v. to come out of
\produce\   v. to create

irony

strapped in safe as produce so to minimize bruising
the number \2\ is somewhat imaginary since they do not belong to you
a magic number
a magic word like *yes*\ or *no*\
two who are the
yes\no

on\off

            i\o

both binary values at the same time

You touch the newspaper on the seat next to you, the one with the picture of Trevor on the front page.

$Nx^y + 2 =$ It has to amount to something. There must me another side to the equation: the logic, which adds up to your existence here, the carpe diem\cogito ergo sum\tabula rasa\Descartes\Rousseau\Trevor

Let P stand for the logic behind your existence here
The argument to make everything significant
But you forgot something which suddenly occurs to you:
The English degree must be included somewhere because you paid for it, and you did all of that work, because having a degree translates to something
And *degree* might be indicated with a small superscripted O just beside the P

\P^o\

or perhaps \P.O.\ which indicates:

    \post office\   ~ n. where deliveries are made

or

    \purchase order\   ~ n. the price you pay

\sin\tax\ = \purchase order\   and the equation has found both sides, it is whole

the logic somehow infinite and perfect

You touch the line on your cheek, trace the spaces around it

Something flashes in the rear-view: An alternative you had not considered

There are police cars pulling in behind you and men running across the rocky outcrop coming toward the car. Quickly, you lean over the steering wheel and twist the key in the ignition.

\a simple function\

You lock the windows, and slide the shifter from *P(ark)* to *N(eutral)* and feel the rolling, forward

\And sorry I could not travel both
\And be one traveller

Softly, you countdown beginning with (5)

> *\five* because it will not be long\
> *\softly* because your voice is hoarse from telling it\

I found a posting online for a small upstart publication in New York called Curbside Quotidian looking for fiction to publish. I had resisted online publication. Certainly, when this story appeared in their first edition in 2011, online publishing wasn't as popular as it has become. The site is now defunct, but it was fun that they published this story.

a space and then a line – this is an image from deep, deep into my childhood. I was riding a country road, doubling with a girl more than twice my age. I was maybe four or five. She was perhaps twelve, burgeoning into adolescence. She had on a brown, fringed bikini. The bike had a long banana seat. As she pedaled with me clinging to her naked midriff, I watched the long, white, intermittent stripes on the roadway. She weaved us back and forth, in and out, between the spaces. I remember thinking how short the lines looked from the car, but how long they were in real life. Everything is different depending on your vantage point. Something I learned from Einstein, a man who knew difficult equations. There was so much wonder wrapped up inside that little head of mine. The places in this story are real, but everything else is fiction.

There are several poetic references here. This includes Stevie Smith, Robert Frost, and then Margaret Atwood, Robert Burns, and William Carlos Williams. Oh, and Sylvia Plath.

In writing and editing this piece, I was less interested in coherent prose than I was in creating the image, the essence of the life being lived. I imagined a deck of Polaroid images. A space and then a line. The peculiarity of using second person point of view (you are here) helps to both disorient and attract. The choice the protagonist makes at the end to shift from *Park* to *Neutral* is interesting to me. Neutral is not a force. By definition, neutral is the lack of inertia. Where the character had spent so much effort trying to reach a (undefined) goal, in the end, she relies on external forces for inertia.

Eva moves deliberately, as though meaning to pass directly through from the kitchen to the bedroom. She stops. Not without intention, but casually, accidentally. She stands at the edge of the living room and touches the back of the brown easy chair they found at the Salvation Army Store so many years ago. Eva watches her husband, lost as he is in the soccer match.

"I kissed you," she says. "Do you remember that?"

"Yes, I remember."

"I kissed you, but it was not the kiss of love."

"I know."

"At the courthouse, later, I kissed you, and *then* I was in love with you."

"I remember," he says. "Why do you repeat this catechism all of the time like I've never heard it?"

"I think you forget."

"I don't forget," he tells her. "You kissed me at the courthouse, and you loved me then."

"No. I love you still."

"I know," he says. "You don't have to remind me all the time."

"You know, I don't remember if you kissed me back," she says, looking for him to see her standing as she is, partially hidden by the furniture and the circumstances. "I kissed you. I loved you, and love you still."

"I know. Now let me watch the match."

The fabric under her hands is still soft, the batting and cushion still resilient.

"When they would rape me, when we were in the prison, I thought of you." She hesitates, knowing that this part is never right, knowing that the words do not mean the right thing. "I didn't think of you because of what they did, but for sadness, because I thought it was terrible for you to have to witness —"

"I know, Eva, I know, and you don't need to describe that to me over and over like this."

"When I think of you in the prison, it is not — it was sadness. I didn't love you then. You were just another prisoner."

"The match, Eva!" He throws up his hands in her direction. "Why do you do this?"

"I need you to know, Ángel, I need you to know that I kissed you later, and then, after, I loved you."

"What is it that you want me to say?"

"Nothing, Ángel. Nothing. I simply want you to know that I thought of you, in your own cell, listening, and that I felt your sadness and not anything else."

"How do you know how I felt?" He still watches the flashes and colours on the small television set.

"Because when I kissed you later, that first kiss of love, I saw your eyes and they have not changed. There is so much of that sadness there, hanging on in you. I have my own scars, Ángel, and you, you have scars too."

"What do you know of my scars? My scars are not like yours," he tells her.

"Exactly. Only you can know your scars. And I can know mine." Eva pauses, adjusts her blouse so that the fabric isn't wrinkled awkwardly across her breast.

"Eva, I don't know why you would compare your suffering with anything I might have felt. They are different."

"I know, Ángel, I know. And this is why I love you: because you understand my scars."

"Now, can I please watch the match?"

Gently, Eva rocks the armchair which is mounted on a swivel base. The springs suddenly make a sound.

"Gabriella is pregnant," she says.

"Again?"

"She is your daughter, Ángel. You should be pleased."

"I was pleased after the first three. Now? Again? I am not pleased."

"How can you say that?"

"She can't support the kids she has already. Four will be a disaster."

"She will be fine."

Eva reaches over the back of the chair and fluffs the small pillow she likes to place under her sore hip when she sits.

"Why are you fussing, Eva? Why don't you sit down?"

"I don't feel like sitting. I'm restless."

"You should watch the match. They're going to lose."

"Nicaragua?"

"Yes, Nicaragua. Panama is going to beat them again."

She steps from behind the chair and considers sitting down with him.

"Do you think about Nicaragua?" she asks.

"I do not think anything about Nicaragua, and neither should you."

"I mean, do you think about *it?*"

"About what? About being in prison? No. I don't think about *it*. I think about Panama winning and Nicaragua losing. I think about soccer, and that is all I think about Nicaragua. Now, Eva, stop your fretting and leave me to watch the match."

"You want me to go?" She steps back.

"Or join me if you like. It doesn't matter." He waves his hand as though swatting at a fly.

Eva looks back toward the kitchen where she has finished the dishes. She glances toward Ángel and then down toward the bedroom where she can see a basket of laundry waiting to be folded.

"I think about *it*," she tells him. "I think about Nicaragua. Not about the prison, but about the courthouse."

"Would you like me to take you somewhere, Eva? Is that it?"

"No."

"After the match. I promise. If you would just leave me in peace. I will take you to the zoo, if you'd like. Or we could take the train to Brooklyn. Or to Manhattan to see the museum. Whatever you would like."

"I want to be with you," she says.

"Well, then sit and watch the match, and *after* we can go somewhere."

"I don't want to go anyway. I just wanted to tell you that I think about the prison. I think about those men, and how their faces seemed so far away."

"I testified against them, didn't I?"

"They were the men you saw raping me?"

"I testified. That is what I just told you."

"But you didn't see them exactly, did you?"

"I saw them in court. That was enough. Men like them, they are all the same and I testified."

"You don't know for sure that it was them?"

"I don't know many things, Eva. I don't even know that Panama will win today."

"Panama always wins against Nicaragua. You said that. You said that it is inevitable," she says.

"There. You know more than me. Maybe I don't need to watch the match. Perhaps you should correct me more often, Eva. Perhaps I'm wrong about a great many things after all."

"You don't have to be sharp with me, Ángel. I was only pointing out –"

"You are always pointing something out, reminding me, informing me. Sometimes, Eva, sometimes I would simply like to enjoy my ignorance. Don't you wish for that sometimes: a bit of ignorance? Don't you want your innocence back?"

"What are you talking about?"

He turns his chair to face her. Behind him, Eva sees that the soccer pitch on television is worn and muddy from the battle. There are only a few green patches remaining.

"When you first saw me, what is it that you saw?"

"That is such a strange question, Ángel. You know exactly the answer."

"Pretend I don't. Now, answer me."

"Of course, I saw your eyes. I saw your beautiful sad eyes through the small slit in the door."

"Very good, Eva. Do you want to know what I saw?"

"Is this a game, Ángel? Are you mocking me?"

"No, Eva. I simply want to tell you what I saw." A noise on the television catches him up for a moment.

"Well, tell me then, Ángel."

"Eva, you saw my eyes, as you have so often told me. You have never asked me. In all of these years, you have never inquired on this one point. You have asked me many other of your tired questions, but never this one."

"You are making me anxious. Can't you simply tell me?"

"You will probably think I am being ridiculous."

"Nonsense." She hesitates. "I can tell that you are serious, Ángel."

"Eva, I saw your destruction."

She shudders, unnerved. "Why would you – "

"And outside of the courthouse, you were already in love with me. How could you love me, when you knew only a small part of me?"

"I know all of you now. I know you have never done me harm. You're a good man, Ángel."

"Let me tell you what I know, Eva. I know how wretched it is to be a man. And I know that it is unfortunate to be a woman."

"That's nonsense, Ángel. You don't even make any sense."

"Do you think so? Listen, man cannot help but sin. And woman cannot be redeemed."

Eva steps back into the hallway, takes another quick look at the bedroom, at the laundry waiting for her. She takes one hand in another for comfort and feels the roughness of her own skin, old, worn. Her husband has turned back to the television.

"Just your eyes, Ángel. For me it was enough. I don't know what else to say. I suppose love is illogical. Love –"

"Love is not illogical," he says, and he turns to her once again. "Love is a great many things. Love is compromise. Love is jealous and angry. Love is disagreement. Love is conditions and abstractions. Love is not illogical. If you'd like to know about *illogical*: violence is illogical. That is something with no rationale at all. War is the same. Torture, even more illogical."

"Why can't I love you for small things, Ángel? If I want to love your eyes, your lips, the nape of your neck, or simply the idea of you, I should be able to do so. Why must everything for you be so grand, so complicated?"

"What happened to us, Eva –"

"I don't know," she tells him.

"It isn't a question."

"What is it then?"

"It is an idea I cannot finish."

Behind him, the television erupts in cheers.

"Who won, Ángel? What is it? What's happened?" She looks past him now where the television is a blur of blue and white celebration.

"Nicaragua," her husband whispers.

"I thought you said —"

Ángel first braces himself as though holding back. She sees the fear in him as she hasn't since the beginning. He rises mechanically from the chair and slowly faces her, rage, exhaustion, and hunger laced across his brow.

"Dammit, woman, have you no brains. I said Panama lost. Panama is lost."

He slams the remote control to the floor. Eva watches the batteries escape under the furniture. She sees his eyes, sudden black pits peering through a small slot in a metal door. She glances to the kitchen where a bulb glows weakly over the stove. In the bedroom there is only laundry to fold.

She touches the cushion again to test the resilience in the batting. "You are right, Ángel. I think that I would rather be blind."

Despite many attempts, this story never found a home. One editor wrote that the dialogue was terse and unnatural. I did not write back that this was deliberate. For one, they are meant to be non-English speakers. I wasn't interested in trying to write with a Spanish accent. Secondly, they are meant to be strangers and would, of course, speak unnaturally to one another. The horror is that, despite their years together, they are still strangers. The dialogue and terse style, indirect as it is, skirting around the truth, is inspired by Ernest Hemingway's Hills Like White Elephants.

The story was also inspired by an interview I heard on CBC radio many years ago. Two people who had been prisoners after a political coup ended up reuniting years later to talk about the ordeal. I imagined those people meeting right after their incarceration and developing a relationship based on their similar experiences. I imagined things not going well.

The door to the back seat is stiff with careless rust. A good yank opens it easily enough. I tell her, I tell Chelsea, just keep the car tidy, I tell her over and over, and then I won't have to clean up after you all the time. Since Henry was born, the debris of life overwhelms her.

Henry's car seat is in the way, so I pull it out and set it on the ground. The crease in the seat behind where the baby sits is ugly: half-eaten fish crackers, unrecognizable bits of mush that might have been apple slices, a collection of Cheerios, stains in the fabric that will never come out. I have work gloves and a garbage bag with me. I scrape at the mess, ashamed that I have let things get this bad.

There is a flash of blue pinched between the seat cushions. The thick leather fingers of the gloves are useless. My own fingers still don't free the treasure. I push a knee down on the seat and finally the blue and red soother rolls down into the crater made by my weight. When he is just new, Henry snoozes on my chest and nurses this thing until I am hypnotized by the sound of his suckling.

When Henry is just old enough to focus, old enough to attend to me, my voice scares him. You talk too loudly, Chelsea says. Your voice is too deep, she says. You have to talk softly. I tell her, don't worry, it's fine. You don't know what you're talking about. A boy can't go around all of his life expecting people to whisper at him. A little while later, I laugh at something he does and instead of giggling, Henry burst into a terrified scream and I know she is right. She gives me a look, but I pretend not to see it. In those early months, I am so afraid of myself, so afraid of his fragility. There are, it seems, more things I can do wrong than right. I try to modulate, to soften my laughter, lighten my intonations. Not baby-talk because I don't believe in that. There is something in the honesty of sleepy children though, and in those tired, whiny, frustrated moments, Henry always reaches for Chelsea. She frowns at me and my regret hangs there between us, unspoken. Chelsea has a way of speaking the boy unconscious. Once asleep, she sometimes passes him to me and then he doesn't seem to mind the smell of me or any of my murmuring.

A bag of pretzels spilled across the back seat. These belong to Henry. In June, we drive up to her parents' cottage. The three of us paddle out to one of the small, uninhabited islands. At first, Chelsea is on me about putting Henry in the canoe strapped into his car seat. It isn't safe, she says. He should have a life jacket. What if we tip? He'll sink. Don't worry, I tell her. She is standing on the dock watching me and I make like I'm ready to paddle away without her. To coax her in, I say, I'm pretty sure they're made to float. I know she doesn't believe me, but Chelsea climbs in anyway, careful not to upset the canoe. The thing about the car seat floating — it isn't true. The water is calm and there is really no reason to worry. Besides, Chelsea leaves me alone about it. We picnic and take pictures all afternoon. It is a brilliant day, all shimmery and wonderful. Henry discovers pretzels; mostly he licks the salt from them and throws the bones to the seagulls. At first, the birds make

Henry nervous, but then he warms to them. Each time one of the birds snatches a soggy pretzel from the beach, Henry giggles, and those small, unbounded laughs echo across the lake. The pretzels on the back seat are stale and soft from having been out of the plastic. I shuffle them into a pile and then into the trash.

On the floor, I find a winter glove, one of a pair I gave to Chelsea at Christmas. There has been an especially healthy snowfall, and the three of us play outside, build a snowman, rub cold noses and share warm kisses. Sometimes everything is just right. Henry is bundled up in his sled in a yellow snowsuit my parents gave him. He tries to follow the snowflakes and only manages to cross his eyes. I keep that picture in my wallet.

Up between the seats, I notice something on the floor that looks familiar, interesting. I move around the car to the passenger side and snatch up the small perfume bottle as I climb in. Accidently, I depress the atomizer with my clumsy gloves. Immediately, Chelsea is in the driver's seat, tropical ginger, laughing and cooing in the rear-view mirror at Henry. She startles me with a smile. I have trouble seeing her like this and she reads my feelings and evaporates.

The perfume is still strong and I have to stumble out of the car to clear my head.

She says, Luke, I need you to drive to the store to get some milk. We're out.

The football game, honey. I point at the television from the sofa. I can't remember if I even look at her.

Then watch Henry, she says, so I don't have to juggle him in and out of the car and the stroller.

He loves car rides, I tell her, and hates football. He'll cry if you go without him, I say, absently, far away so that she thinks I am already missing her.

We need milk, she says again.

I can go later, I tell her, honestly distracted this time by someone injured on the field, players huddled nearby, officials and a gurney running out to rescue him. She is already out of the room. I could have watched him. I was only being playful.

Perhaps I will find forgiveness for not being more to her if only I can fill in the gaps where I have been absent. This is the thing, really, the thing I want to find: some fragment to show her that I am here for her. The empty Starbucks coffee cup resting in the console – not mine. The collection of coins in the ash tray – not mine. The warped cardboard parking pass from the college hanging from the mirror – not mine. I am missing. Here is another thing she should have taken out of the car: a magazine, dog-eared, sun-bleached, and damp with neglect. Parenting tips. Recipes. Weight loss advice. Why do you waste your time reading this stuff? She tells me, I like the articles. They entertain me. Sometimes, there are some good ideas. I won't buy any more magazines if you don't want me to, she says defensively. I tell her, I tell Chelsea, do what you want. I don't want to be that guy that doesn't support his wife. You just don't need, you don't need any help being better than you are. She is absolutely perfect. Chelsea is as beautiful a mother as anyone I can imagine, if only a little messy.

I find a green crayon on the dashboard up near the odometer. I don't know how such a thing has found itself there, separated from the other colours. I squeeze it in my hand. The paper around the wax has little teeth marks. I told her parents he was too young for colouring. I watch Henry tear the newsprint pages from the colouring book and gum the crayons. Here on the seat, there is a long strand of red hair and I pull the gloves off for this one. It's just a hair, but this is no place for it. I don't know where it belongs, but not here. Certainly, not here.

I remember one of the things I was going to look for. The driver's seat has been pushed all the way back. I lean down and squeeze the mechanism to shift the seat forward. I reach behind me for the crushed package tucked down on the floor of the back seat. Chelsea bought a cute pair of white leather walking shoes for Henry. He hasn't worn them yet. He has only just started to stand on his own. The smell of leather is rich and clean. With the gloves still off, I take time, hold each shoe carefully in my hands; I fit my fingers inside one of them. I tuck the shoes back in, wrapped in paper, and then struggle the bruised lid back onto the box and set it beside me.

At the morgue, the assistant funeral director washes their bodies. I imagine this is what he does because at the service the caskets are both open. The boxes are deep and I do not look in. One is smaller than the other, and this one, this one, I can't even look at it. I stay across the room. Someone has removed the pine lids and tucked the two coffins close together so mother can be with son.

There is an uncomfortable sofa and I fall into it, nearly collapse. I study the faded fabric, the plain carpet, the black shoes filing past me. Across from where I sit, on the wall, there is a television set. My mother points it out when she brings me a cup of coffee. I wave her off. Chelsea and Henry are together on the screen, a picture I took at the beach in June. Some of the seagulls are behind them in the shot fighting over pretzels. Here Chelsea is alone, sitting on the steps outside our apartment, still pregnant. This is Henry in his stroller, bundled in and safe. Here they are in bed together when he was still nursing. There is no marker to indicate that I was holding the camera for every single image. There is no banner scrolling across the wide monitor to explain that I was there the whole time.

The mess is bigger than me; I'm willing to admit that now, willing to swallow the guilt, let it go so that I can leave what needs to be left. The soiled medical rags on the floor, a piece of twisted metal I don't recognize, some broken glass I can't identify. I climb out of the car with the baby shoes. I have gathered the green crayon, the perfume bottle, and the long red hair. They are all inside the box. I leave the coins. I leave the garbage bag too, the work gloves.

The voice in my head tells me not to look back. I wish I had the strength to stop myself, to force myself blindly away. Yet, there is a thing I long for, a thing that I cannot find. Suddenly, she is there again: Chelsea in the driver's seat down at the end of the laneway, slowly backing out into traffic. I still have the TV remote in my hand and I can see her making eyes at Henry in the rear-view mirror to calm him. Maybe she flashes him a smile. She doesn't see me. I call to her more and more loudly, I'll go, I'll go, I'll go. Running down the pavement in my bare feet, waving, stop, stop, stop. She doesn't hear me any more than she sees the truck coming. It's just milk. It's only milk. She flashes a worried look to me as I race across the wrecker's yard and land in the passenger's seat to be with her. By the time I reach the car, she is gone again. The baby too.

Slowly, I cross the yard out toward where I parked my sister's van. There is a sign on the gate that warns to never mind the dog but beware the owner. I hug the shoebox to my chest. These are the only pieces left. Not enough to bring them back or let them go; just the scatter of things gone wrong.

I wrote *Missing Pieces* twice. One of my daughters read the first incarnation and found it predictable and not very interesting. Indeed, I had written it with this *gotcha* ending that was terrible. I turned her comments over and rewrote. I made the deaths more obvious and predictable. The first draft was about plot and devise, which is never the way to write. This later draft is about the character and thematically about regret. Sometimes the small decisions we make will break us.

Perhaps because of the horror of it, I've never found a publisher for the tale. Another story which includes the death of a child. Some publishers actually include a clause that they will not accept stories about children in peril.

As he clings to the jagged edges of the icy hole, Bill feels his new snowshoes dangling like great heavy holiday plates at the end of his legs. The snowshoes arrive as a Christmas gift only two days ago.

The pond is no more than a swamp stranded in the hydroelectric easement behind the subdivision. As he drops, he expects to fall only as deep as his knees. There is time to feel disgust at having to trudge home, humiliated, cold, the snowshoes ruined, mucky, and wet. Instead, the descent is absolute. He flounders, his fingers clawing at the ice trying to keep his head above water. His elbows dig in like blunt talons, his hands already too cold to do the job.

Bill has never wandered down here before today. The sign that marks the trail names the area Wyndham Park. There is a path which weaves around the weeds, over a hummock, and back down behind the high school. In the summer there are wild calla lilies, cattails, and woodsy little owls which haunt the slough like spooky trolls. The path is never paved because, during the summer, when the lilies bloom and the owls call, and the cattails sough in the breeze, the hollow simply screams with mosquitoes, mites, and the unpleasant stagnant punk which rises in gassy bursts from the bog. Bill smells it now, steaming up through the hole he has made in the ice like nature's winter fart.

No one thinks of dying, especially not like this. Perhaps in palliative care at the end of a long life, or in the ambulance with sirens howling about your head on the way to the hospital after a terrible crash. But not like this, alone in the dark – and especially not during the holidays with family waiting at home.

Eight minutes. He reads it somewhere. Maybe he heard it in a movie. Eight minutes is how long you can expect to survive in icy waters before you die of hypothermia or before the madness and pain draw you under. The only other Christmas present he receives – this one from his wife – is a wristwatch. As he opens the small package, she explains how she has paid extra for one that is shock and water proof. Today, the device has endured both and the cheery green glow shines up at him. At least two minutes already gone. Bill struggles himself into an exhausted wheeze. Clearly, he thinks, I am not getting out of this one.

Sharon is back at the house clearing dishes from dinner and entertaining Ryan, their wayward son. Ryan, an English teacher, has made a special trip back from South Korea for the holidays with his new girlfriend, a woman apparently named Anne Young. Bill isn't sure about the name. That is how the introduction sounds to Bill, and over the past few days he mumbles her name rather than saying it outright in case he gets it wrong and offends.

For Bill, it seems as though he and his neighbour Gary have spent the entire summer talking about Christmas. Both want ATVs. They discuss various models as they hose down their shared driveway. Gary fixates on the Manticore, a monstrous machine that would best a car on a quarter-mile dirt track. Bill would be happy with a smaller model, just something big enough to tootle through the hydro easement. Gary is determined that he will get the one he wants, even if he has to buy the thing himself. Bill admits that his best chance is to leave hints for his wife. As autumn casts her leaves before winter, Bill clips pictures out of a flyer and tucks them beside Sharon's coffee on the kitchen table. He hasn't seen Gary in a month, since the cold shut them both in. For a week now, Gary's car has been parked in the driveway rather than in the small garage. Bill thinks that Sharon, clever as she is, has negotiated a hiding place for his Christmas present.

When he wakes on Christmas morning, Bill stands at the front door in his pyjamas and boots, coffee in hand, waiting for the others to wake. He stares at the empty driveway, anticipating. Instead of leading him outdoors, Sharon beckons him to the tree in the front room. The little box is blue, and that is supposed to mean something about the quality. The dandy new wristwatch is inscribed, *with love, Sharon.* He kisses her dryly. Ryan doesn't wrap the snowshoes in anything more exciting than a Walmart bag. Still the gift is a big step for a son who left home as an angry young man. When Bill asks Ryan when he is going to settle down and move closer to home, Christmas disintegrates into a tense and silent breakfast.

Four minutes. It might be all he has left. Bill wonders how to use his remaining time in some useful activity. He might call out. The house is just there beyond the trees. He can see light spilling from the back window. Ryan, Sharon, or even Anne Young might pass by and hear him calling from the darkness of the swamp like some old monster lost out on the moor. But the snow has a way of culling the sound. Bill marvels at how the gasping sounds cling to his face.

"Listen, Buddy," Gary says. "Anytime you wanna ride it, she's yours. You don't need to ask." Bill watches Gary circling his new ATV. The shimmering machine roars hungrily. Bill believes that there never will come a time when he will cross the driveway and knock on Gary's door and ask for the keys. Bill knows he should have bought himself his own ATV.

"She got it for you, eh?"

"You betcha," Gary says. "You know, Buddy," He halts his tour around the bike and wraps a big arm around Bill's shoulder too amicably. "I knew she would. Didn't I tell you so?" Gary squeezes him until it hurts.

Bill pulls away from the man who smells too early of eggnog and rum. When Gary circles the machine again, Bill realizes that his neighbour is afraid of climbing into the wide seat. There are three more nervous tours around the vehicle. Gary points out the fuel tank, the splashguards and even comments on the nubby tires. Bill thinks that Gary's wife might just as readily have gift-wrapped an eighteen year-old girl. The man is all eyes and no action.

"I don't know where I'll ride it."

"You should try the pond," Bill says. There's a trail back there. Nobody uses it. I don't know why you couldn't ride this thing back there."

"Hey, that's just the place." Gary's face lights up.

"The snow is not too deep yet. And the pond is frozen."

"You want to take it for a ride? I mean, after I've tried it?"

"No, I'm fine. I got the snowshoes." Bill can't help smiling. He thinks of the eighteen year-old and the ATV in the same thought. Gary will never truly saddle either horse. He may ride the machine, but he will never own it. The thing is bigger than his neighbour. In a metaphorical way. "I got snowshoes," he repeats.

His elbows and bare fists strain to keep him elevated at least partway out of the water. As the last light of day cuts down the horizon, Bill watches a small shadow race to catch a falling leaf. Through the prism of a single drop of ice clinging to a branch, Bill watches the light turn green, and then blue, and then purple. He thinks that purple might be the colour of his toes. The cold begins to bite each one of them off. Purple. Even in the muffled silence of the swamp, God might hear him shouting out in sharp, desperate breaths. He has need of a bigger miracle than God might visit upon a lonely ogre stranded in a stinking bog. Broken pieces of ice float around him collecting frosty little stars at their edges. Bill draws in a staccato of tight breaths and hauls his leg up impossibly against the weight of his wet clothes and cold, aching muscles. He manages to slide one snowshoe up out of the water and unto the ice. The ragged crust snaps like an old dry bone and his leg rolls back into the water while a large chunk of ice summersaults beside him growing the hole.

It is the last energy he has. This should be over, he thinks, and soon the tremendous weight of the cold will sink me into the sediment. In his mind, Sharon is drying a tea cup, standing in the back hallway where she has wandered to look for him. Like a faithful dog, she waits for the back door to open, for him to return. She reaches for the knob and wonders if Bill is playing a prank. Bill imagines Ryan as he considerately lifts himself from the sofa, abandoning the game console that has cost Bill three hundred dollars, but which seemed a necessary gift for a prodigal son. He thinks of Ryan hurrying to cradle his mother who erupts into a sudden panic. "There, there, mother," Ryan whispers. "Dad's enjoying the mild evening. That's all. Nothing to worry about."

Bill finds tears despite the painful shivers crushing his body. It will be Ryan who wanders out into the cold later wearing borrowed boots from the back closet. It will be Ryan who recognizes the mound in the middle of the pond and flies back across the yard to call for help. It will be Ryan who will not recover from this. It doesn't seem fair.

Over turkey and cranberries, Anne Young sets out four thimble-sized glasses and fills each one with a hearty liquid the deep crimson colour of blood. Anne slides a brimming thimble across the tablecloth, and her long fingers touch his with a shock. He feels the warmth and strange energy of her fingertips across the linen. When each of them has a drink, she raises hers and announces "Gonna Pay" and empties her glass. Bill isn't sure he has heard it right, but he lifts his glass and answers merrily, "Gonna Pay you too!"

From the look in Ryan's dark eyes Bill knows that he has said it wrong. Anne Young is smiling at him, but it isn't real. It is a smile to placate, a smile to apologize for assuming too much, or trying too hard. The liquid fills him with such heat that Bill is certain he has been poisoned, like Claudius, or Nero: tyrants at their bitter end. When the heat grows, and even Ryan is hacking from the choking grip of the wine, Bill relaxes a little. Still, Sharon and Anne Young sit across the table, watching the two men with hungry and unsettling curiosity.

Bill had really not meant to protest, but South Korea is so far away. There are teaching jobs all over the place, even here in town. But, South Korea? And Sharon had done nothing to stop him. That is the thing, isn't it? She just let him go, and then someone was *gonna pay*. That is how this works: everyone does what they want, but eventually everything has a cost. Someone always pays. Bill slides his empty thimble across the table hoping for a refill. Anne Young's smile wavers, and Bill pulls his hand back across and tucks it under his leg.

He pays now, with terrible, paralyzing cold. Bill is barely able to gulp little breaths, his fingernails bent back bloody against the ice; an itch drills into his spine which he can neither reach nor scratch. Around him, the swamp groans. It sounds like settling, but it could be waking up. A silence follows and then another loud percussion hammers across the ice. In this version of things, he tells Sharon that he'll be home before dark. He can't remember if this is true. In another twenty minutes she will ask Ryan to go looking. In another twenty minutes, Bill thinks, I will be a looming hulk slumped on the edge here. If Ryan puts her off, clinging as he might to the new video games, it will be an hour before the boy gets up to pee and maybe then attend to his mother. In that time, Sharon might try to distract her worry with a book or a magazine. In this version, Sharon might still call out, tentatively, wondering where he has gone. It is a quiet enough night that he might hear her the first time if she calls out right now. But he doesn't have the breath to call back to her. His lungs feel all shrunken and tired, worn out from gulping for air.

Not like this. Not at the holidays. It doesn't seem fair.

There might only be a few minutes. And then what? What is death exactly when it comes like this, in closing increments? Bands of darkness begin twisting around his periphery, stars exploding where stars have never appeared in the suburb before. Death is probably like birth – just a thing that happens; a sliding from one realm to another. A small change. Slipping from here to there. No protest, no complaint. That is all it is. Just a slipping. Slight, apologetic, yet sincere.

Ryan is standing there in the doorway. Bill pulls him into a hug, awkwardly, and he wants to keep holding on, to never let go, to dig his fingers in and just hold on. But Bill feels how embarrassing his affection is for Ryan and quickly releases. Then Anne Young is there in the doorway and before this strange witness to his selfish love, the shame is worse.

There are no tears left. All he can manage is a few staggered breaths through his nostrils. He catches puffs of steam escaping, sloughing off the bit of heat still left. The last thing he needs right now is this relentless wristwatch to count down the moments. Who needs a damn waterproof watch, anyway? *I don't even like swimming*, he thinks. Sharon never could get things right. She is always saying the wrong thing, intimating something other than what needs to be said. She let Ryan run off to Asia and bought me a stupid wristwatch instead of an ATV. And Ryan wants me to lose weight – that is what the message is in the snowshoes. I am too heavy for him. Too heavy probably for Sharon.

There are no more shivers. No aches. Bill feels comfortable in his wretched pool, a lumbering giant. I'm too heavy for this life. Bill strains to see the wristwatch, tries to find the second hand, but the light sputters like an old motel sign, like a dying firefly. He sees the time. One minute. Only one minute left. But it hasn't been eight minutes, has it? Not according to the wristwatch. Twenty-seven minutes have dragged by. Sharon is resting on the couch, her feet tucked under her son's leg for warmth. They are laughing together watching Ryan play video games. Laughing. Anne Young is making some sort of tea to warm them up against the cooling of the night. Bill imagines her in the kitchen. She is wearing his slippers. The ones Sharon gave him last year for Christmas when he wanted something else. But *something else* flounders in the fog of forgetfulness.

Suddenly, from across the swamp, Bill hears a rumbling that is ominous and familiar. The twin headlights of Gary's Manticore pitch across the embankment which slopes into the cattails, lilies, and then down to the ice. The machine lurches on the crest. There is a pause, and Bill is blinded by the intense whiteness of the light. The engine stills a moment. The lights dim and blink as though struck by sudden recognition. Gary's voice rises across the bog: "Hold on, Buddy, I'm coming." It is the voice of God calling from His chariot of fire.

Bill would like to answer, would like to tell him to stop where he is, to go home and get help. Bill would like to call to his idiot neighbour to tell him not to bother, that his family has forgotten him already, I'm gonna pay, gonna pay, it's okay, go away, but the engine roars back to life and the light bounces quickly toward him. Then, suddenly, the whole mess dips horribly and the entire wreck is swallowed, choking, sputtering below the ice. Meters from Bill, a great dark mass remains, while Gary thrashes, howling into the night like a harpy, and all around the swamp, kitchen lights are glowing on. Bill can see Gary more clearly now, can see that he is too heavy for the minutes clawing at him, can see the blueness of his eyes. Bill tries to cup another puff of air into his lungs. He tries to whisper across the chasm for Gary to stop. Eight more minutes together and then all of this will be over.

Swamp Thing first appeared in From the Depths, a beautiful online and print publication. The story was published in the summer of 2012.

When writing, I often choose names for characters deliberately. Sometimes, they name themselves. For example, Ryan's girlfriend is not really named Ann Young. "Anyoung" means "hello" in Korean. I'm not sure any reader needs to understand this, but it was funny to me that Bill would misunderstand her name as he misunderstands so much in his life.

I read or heard something about how long a person could survive after falling through the ice. I imagined what it might be like in the moments after you resign yourself to your fate. What would someone think about? What would that experience be like? Would you finally be honest with yourself? Would your true character emerge? I hope there's some humour in this story. I very much intended it to be funny. You might have to re-read it to find the jokes. As badly as I feel for poor Bill's situation, I can't get the desperate image out of my head of this man not really getting that he is the monster.

Over Her Perfect White Shoulder

She stands over there under the dormer by the window in her bra and panties waiting for me. She looks down into the street fretting like a sailor's widow. I am inside, over here by the door watching her as she waits. When she glances over her shoulder, she can't see me because I am now – and she is twenty years ago.

I tell her I have to go, that I have to cool off because I want her too badly.
Don't kill yourself, she says, because she knows I mean to.
I tumble down the stairs from the loft where she will wait such a long, long time for me to find her again. It is a room tucked up under the roof so that the ceiling very nearly makes a triangle where there are only two appropriate postures:
a) standing here where I am now, watching her
b) over there in the corner on your knees

The only other space for standing is under the dormer there where she

where the roof line breaks away
from the perfect geometry.

I never go over there. If I am over there, I am out on the roof.

Don't kill yourself, she says again.

I call back with silence from the bottom of the stairs. I have a pocket full of Tylenols that I have been popping like PEZ all day. The streetcar down Queen to the beach is crowded. Every time I want a pill I pretend to yawn. After a while this is just funny so I start making it more and more obvious until the people around move away from me. Eventually it looks like this:

a) I yawn hippopotamus wide
b) I laugh
c) I pop a PEZ/pill into my mouth

The effect is tectonic. Soon I have all kinds of room around me, like I'm an island. Every time the streetcar lurches to a stop, I lunge, as though I might slide over Asia or crash into Africa. I think about how outrageous it is that I left her standing there in her bra and panties. I could have turned us into a continent. Instead, I am an island on the TTC. The Woodbine Racetrack used to be here but it moved to Rexdale. Rather than change names to match the new environs, it is still the Woodbine Racetrack. I don't understand why they didn't change the name. Instead of yawning again, I point to the place where the track used to be and I ask Asia and Africa, but they only slide further away from me. I tell them that maybe someone thought the vagabonds would wander out there in search of something impossible: a treasure, a memory of better times. I imagine the parking lot of the Rexdale Mall turned to a shanty town. It is like a prairie of grey concrete out there. I yawn again.

I spill into the street with a number of other islands and we move away from each other in the dark. I'm wearing an overcoat I borrowed from Dostoyevsky and a shirt so thin and cold that it rattles against my skin. I don't really know my way around this neighbourhood, but I follow a smell that should not belong to a lake.

The beach is night because it is grey. The slippery sand doesn't slow my desert boots. In fact, there is no angst-filled moment of poignant reflection when I pause to consider my desperate mortality or the many loves that I have lost or the emptiness of my pockets. I am twenty years ago now and this is a deliberate march out into the cold February blackness to find Stevie Smith or Maggie Atwood at the bottom of the lake. But I am not waving, and I am not drowning, and I am not a photograph caught in the silt of the murky depths. I wade into water as deep as my waist with the waves pounding against the rest of me. I feel very little of anything at all. I expected something different.

Back up on the beach, someone is calling to me and I turn to find a man we both know. He has only followed me here because bra and panties probably begged him to do so. I am in the loft and he is in the basement. Strangers are on the main. There is a cat in the yard that belongs to none of us but gets fed anyway.

I trudge back out of the water to confront him.
Why are you here? I don't need you.
I'm not here for you, he says. I don't care about you. I'm here for her.
Well, you should go back to her then. She's your sister, right?
You're a narcissist, do you know that? You only love yourself.

Now, if you were in my place, you may very well have done one of the following:
a) told him off
b) sworn him down
c) lathered him in insults

Of course, I, I take the road less travelled, and that has made all the difference, right? I keep my mouth shut, turn and jog back down toward the water before he tackles me and punches me hard in the face three times until I stop laughing. Nobody can love me. That is what I determine in this moment, with him astride my chest.

Of course, I go back to her. There is very little else I can do. Apparently, I could not kill myself. She is someone to hurt because she is already hurting. She walks as though there are thumbtacks pushing up through the bottom of her Jesus sandals and she is learning to tolerate my disease. I know she thinks of me like this:
a) at least it's a relationship
b) I have nowhere else to go
c) maybe he'll change, everyone changes

I know she is losing confidence that she can change me. I am her brightest hope, which is like fingernails bitten to the quick. She is someone to remember because she is so full of pain. She glances over her perfect white shoulder and I know that no one will ever see me as she does: weak, afraid. I hide all that, but she sees me. The fact that she ignores what she sees

what she sees she sets aside. That is what I tell myself twenty years ago, but now, now over her perfect white shoulder I see everything as she did and I am failing. I am deaf from the sound of arguing in my head.

And so I stand here, watching her waiting for me. The room is blue. Van Gogh blue. I guess it is blue like any artist goes blue. Twenty years ago, there was a futon there, over there in the corner where I slept on the floor like a Bohemian with one pillow and one cold sheet. I wish it was there now because I would throw myself down and smell her sweat and her hair gel on the pillow. She is a nail that drives right through me. A guilt that will not be redeemed.

The house is for sale. The sign out front has been there for some months, but, like a place haunted, it will not sell. Her legs are white as teeth, her breasts well-formed and even. It is the only memory I have of her, debased and degraded like this, body parts, like scenes from an accident, her confessions raw, her nerves wracked with the neglect I've given her. She sees me though, and I can't stand what she sees. She stands there looking down at the street and I have a habit lately of placing thumbtacks inside my shoes.

She does not fade for me like some memories do. I stand here at the Open House, the real estate agent busy downstairs with a different couple. I am twenty years later, perhaps a little longer than that, and currently, freshly jettisoned from another relationship. It is the same refrain, like a boatman's dirge, returning over and over again to the unforgiving and treacherous, traitorous seas. Another marriage too long in the doldrums. This time even the children are marooned so that I may properly tend to this cancer and the old ghost who will not let me be. Her fragile scrutiny follows me even when I run from it.

I have a pocket filled with more expensive medicine this time – Xanax, Cipralex – and the pills are only just beginning to take the edge off. My other pocket rattles with coins and next I am going down to the harbour to dredge the lake for some old poets. I decide not to bother with the streetcar. Instead, I march to the dock for the island ferry and jump right in. I'm laughing when I do it so the few people waiting there think it's some sort of lark. I wave this time, and some of the children wave back before their parents shift to guard their hands less I entice them in. But there is something that happens before

> just before I jump the barricade into the lake my phone rings
> and it always happens like this:
> a) she turns her head over her perfect white shoulder
> b) she sees what she sees
> c) and I know it

But it isn't her this time. It's the wife I just left, or who left me. And I can't help thinking that something about me must beg these women to save me when I don't want or need saving at all. And I tell her:

> I told you not to call.
> It isn't me. Lucinda wants to talk to you.
> Women do this. Make the children say what they cannot.
> What is it? What does she want?
> I hear her in the background. *Does he want to talk to me, Mommy?*
> Hi Daddy. When are you coming home?
> I will not lie to a child. Not yet.
> I think you need to talk to Mommy about that.
> Will you bring me a kitty? Daddy? *Is he still there, Mommy?*

I think of the stray that lived behind that old loft place and survived on cans of tuna fish, stale Kraft Dinner, and leftover Hamburger Helper.

> Lucinda, give the phone back to Mommy.

I'm going to tell wife number three to buy the cat, but she hangs up instead.

I quit my job. Number one rule of self-destruction: make the money go away.

There is money. Wife number one never asks about it. Wife number two doesn't care, she just wants out. This one asks enough questions about all kinds of things so that I can usually skip the tricky ones. There is a lot of money buried. I don't need it, but it's there.

> I have a black marker in my pocket.
> I write a bank account number on my arm.

The water isn't cold enough to shock me into hypothermia or a heart attack, so I have to swim. Toronto Island isn't far enough away, maybe just enough, but still, I know that somewhere between here and there an instinct will kick in and pull me the distance even if I really want it some other way. I will be forced to climb up the shore, past the docks, the yachts, the boats, the clever tourists in their white shorts and shades, walk around the amusement park, cross a road, past mailboxes, Adams, Gilmartin, Clyde, in white cracked paint, a swimming pool for a short chlorine rinse, and then to the other end of the island where there are cottages and the smell of goose turd is the only thing stronger than the lake. There, I will walk out to the end of a short dock, maybe interrupt a barbeque, and jump back in. I know that out there, in the middle of the lake, there is a shipping channel where the water is deep and black and cold. No poets there. That is where I will finally tire and any instinct will fail me and my bloated body will drift toward the St. Lawrence with my last will and testament inked on my arm in nervous black scrawl.

Here is what happens:
a) I will be reported missing
b) the bank will drill into my safety deposit box
c) they will find the instructions:
d) use the money to buy the house with the blue loft
e) burn it to the ground

Then even my youngest daughter, Lucinda, even she will know me thin as paper, frail as a flower. Then she can hate me as boldly as all the rest. Every green putrid wave glances over a perfect white shoulder. Still she sees me, still I can't help looking at her hoping she will see me differently. Or, that both of us will go blind.

This character is very unpleasant. Perhaps more so because the story is written in first person POV. He is greasy and sleazy. A racist, narcissist, and misogynist. I wish the entirety of this piece was fiction, but there's an ancient version of me dressed in an overcoat drifting down to the beach. I really did go out there one night and expected to freeze to death. In the time before cell phones, I was fortunately apprehended by a friend who was concerned for my well-being. He never hit me, and I never made it to the beach.

Like Prisoners, this story ends with a desire not to see the inevitable horror. I tell people I write horror. But the horror isn't always in the prose. Sometimes it's already happened, as in A Very Small Stain, or might yet happen, as in Prisoners. In this story, the horror starts in a blue apartment in the 1980s (maybe even earlier) and never stops.

If we can't write or read about the things we hate, we can't move past them. There is a reference near the end to John Cheever's The Swimmer. The names on the mailboxes and the dip in the pool are stolen from Cheever's story.

These are the broad strokes. The finer detail looks like this: a paint-by-number. The kind with the brush that is too plush and the little oily paint pots which run out or dry up before the artwork is complete. This is what he looked like to me: washed out and never quite finished: A net of scratchy blue lines betray the image of a much greater man. He talked and talked and said the same thing over and over again, justifying himself always, but never clarifying the picture. Daddy was never wrong. This is different than suggesting that he was always right. He would have argued with my semantics, but for me the variation is important.

In the chaos of all of his talking I would like to say that I managed to master my own independent language. The truth is that I'm not that confident. He died before I was twelve and by then I was so used to his way of seeing the world that I missed the numbers, the blue lines, the outline of what really is. I missed all of the details and simply painted the world the way I wanted it to look like. Or how I imagined he thought I thought it should look.

Died is wrong too. He disappeared on a fishing trip. He didn't even like fishing. He had to get away, and away is where he got to. Northern Ontario is all lakes and trees. Somewhere among that mess his putrid corpse wants to be validated and identified correctly. The Provincial Police looked. They circled lake after lake, sometimes by boat, sometimes by helicopter. I followed the search on the news until it faded in the public eye, until we had to call to find out the latest reports, until they called off the search and winter set in.

We held a funeral late into the desolation of January. For me it was confusion. People wept, drank, wept some more. I sat around waiting for him to come through the door and tell us we were all wrong, boast that he had survived, had walked out of the woods and that some one of us should have looked further, hung on longer. I felt dread mixed with guilt that it might actually be possible. Part of me wished it to be so. I imagined him beating his chest, looking down at me, disappointed, upsetting my hair with his cold, callused fingers. Instead, every time the door opened, it was another worried relative with a tissue balled in one hand and a casserole in the other.

***

I had excused myself from English class to find out about art school, about moving and launching out on my own. Instead I was confronted by this parapsychologist with the timing and tact of a nosebleed. The guidance counsellor asked me how it felt when *he* disappeared and for a moment I thought I was imagining because it was none of her business. She tapped her pencil. Looked at me, but not directly. Started saying something and then moved the cursor on her computer screen. Opened an email. Closed it again. Crossed and uncrossed her legs. Then it just spilled out.
"Was it strange for you? I mean, when *he* disappeared."
"Who?" I didn't need to ask, but neither did she.
"Oh, I'm sorry." She blushed.
"My father? Is that who you mean?"
Yes."
He had been gone for almost six years, and I was graduating in six months. I had other things on my mind. I had done a fine job at setting Daddy and all of his weight aside. I didn't answer the guidance counsellor. My Daddy issues were all resolved.

The men in my life let me down, disappoint. Insipid, weak, failing. At first it was just Daddy, but there were others. Momma was lonely and her suitors were evidence of the frailties of men. She remarried, but that didn't last very long – eight months, maybe.

Her number three smelled always of sawdust and sourness. I never dared ask either of them why. Momma seemed entranced by him. Cary was his name. Like an ancient actor my mother remembered. A feminine name to me. He was altogether more settled, more sympathetic than number two. He touched me one night and that was the end of number three. Don't get close.

At college, I fall into photography which is more exciting, rhythmic, and satisfying than line drawing. There is immediacy to the lens that I come to prefer. I stick a notice up in the common room of the dorm asking for male models. I find a couple of gay exhibitionists. After that, a shy kid doing self-therapy and reading Russian classics. Then, a wanderer with a soft jawline and bangs that fall over his eyes. The exhibitionists make me smile, but the images aren't very good. The shy kid insists on posing with his teddy bear and won't take off his headphones. The wanderer and I hit it off. At first, I'm telling him where to stand, what to do, but before sunset, he has my Nikon, and I'm covering my face, awkward, giggling, never a beauty.

Even though I've read about these kinds of things, I still have room to be shocked when I wake up one night with a boot on my face. Love is a terrible mythology. I think there is no such thing as love. I think there is clinging. I think there is desperation. I don't think there is more than that. Noise and smell and sweat in the dark. The false appreciation that hangs around waiting for more and then getting angry when there are conditions, when it gets real. Don't feel pain when it happens. Save it for later and feel it by yourself. Don't trust either.

The lens searches for the symbols, decorations, artifacts we use to prop ourselves up. I am the cucumber watcher in search of evidence of things not seen. The watcher inhabits a shack in a field of cucumbers. The watcher keeps the plants safe from thieves. I suppose thieves. Goats or rabbits or other vermin might have been a threat. But cucumbers! Cucumbers grow like weeds. Cucumbers have no need of watchers. I reason that unwatched cucumbers grow into bitter yellow gourds. Unwatched cucumbers make themselves inedible, without need of watching. Perhaps the watcher is there to catch the fruit before the yellowing. I am too late to the scene. In the lens, I frame graffiti and garbage in alleyways, spray painted philosophies, atrocities, orgies, logos, dreams. Dregs. Flotsam. Detritus. Everyone is lonely. Everyone is grieving, yellow. Beyond hope. My mother, Old Testament loving atrocity that she was, recounts the tale of the cucumber watcher. It becomes a mantra for her every time I leave the house as an adolescent: "Don't be the cucumber watcher." She means not to waste my life, not to become a nothing who has no other place than a shack in a farmer's wasted field. Despite her need for greasy men in her life to cling to, I don't think she understands the innuendo. Cucumber watcher. I suppose anything she might have said to my leavings might have crossed my mind as sexual. Adolescence has a filter in that direction, doesn't it?

***

The law of absolutes is that a thing either is, or it isn't. There is pain or no pain, there is nothing in between. Black or white. But mostly a bloated, disgusted yellow. There is love or there is no love. When he raped me, this is what I worked out in my head. There is only now. There is no sense in anything nostalgic. If there is therapy of any kind, it is working out the days ahead, not re-evaluating the past or justifying disabilities. Head down, moving forward. That is the strength of Sisyphus. (I imagine him pushing a yellow, weeping, bulbous cucumber up a hill). This moment, unwatched, alone, the moment after the rape, this is the one that frees me, allows me to move forward. After Bernt, the wanderer-model with the soft jaw, the liar, the tyrant with his boot in my face, after he leaves, there is only yellow.

No man in my life has ever been anything more than poison. These are the details, well inside the broad strokes now, the micro-bits of what I've figured out. There are no little blue lines showing through on the canvas. There is only the jaundice paint and it is pushed on heavy. Stroke after stroke of colour so that nothing below bleeds through. I photograph the dust, the threads fallen from the mattress, the grout separated from the glass. A bit of mould on old cheese. This is how we destroy the self we do not tolerate. Find a detail and enlarge it until it is *inedible*, unrecognizable as the thing it once was. Destroy its context until all meaning is robbed from it. Illuminate the meaningless because the masquerade is all there is.

The photographs of graffiti cover the walls of my small apartment. I send them like canaries, a few at a time, to magazines, galleries, to try to get some attention. To fight for survival. I know they're mimetic. The original is not mine, not even my idea. But it is the framing that matters. Ceci n'est pas une pipe. Or R. Mutt's urinal. Who can forget Warhol? Charlatan and plagiarist. I am not the first to copy, reframe, or celebrate the discovery of something found or refound. I am not the first to hurt or the first to lose either. There is art and there is anti-art.

I am sitting up in bed, propped on pillows, alone. My laptop is open and the machine pings that I have a new message. I read it quickly, run to the bathroom, throw up.

It shouldn't be this way, of course. I know it. I know it intellectually like I know there are equations bigger than me. I know it and still it shocks me. Not every man should be a tyrant, just like not every woman should love a fascist. I forget the rest of the syllogism, but in its final state it must add up to something reasonable. Not every man should be a tyrant and therefore…

Therefore, what?

Therefore, I type a terse response to the email and try to soften it with a smiley face. I erase that and start again, trying to be less terse. But how can I be anything else but terse? It's Daddy. He isn't dead. He has been alive this whole time. Lost in self-doubt, he writes. *Lost in self-absorption*, I think. Lost in *only-one-person-in-your-universe*, I think. So what? What is it I'm supposed to respond with? Pity? Congratulations? Sudden adulation? I have come to hate the masochists: Magritte, Picasso, Pollock. Those arrogant bastard undoers! There isn't a language, not a grammar for this sort of thing. A whole new syntax is required to try to communicate like this. Alive. I think about *alive* over and over again as I watch my fingers fly and then erase over and over again. *Wrong Jennifer*, I type at least once, yet backspace that too. It's not this iteration of Jennifer that is wrong, after all. It's the Roberts, the R. Mutts, the Marcel Duchamps. The spoilers. The unwatchers. The Pollocks. The Picassos. It's everything down the toilet in one horrible swallow. If I broke apart, would I have the patience to patch all that glass back together again? It's the *missing-presumed-dead* that turns out to be all wrong.

Three years of uncomfortable art college. Four years of painful high school before that. Ancient, excruciating middle school. All that time, he might have been watching me, sharing a bus shelter, sleeping by the dorm building under a slice of cardboard big enough for a roof. Watching me as I yellow. Bloat. Come apart. Things have a tendency to fall apart more than they come together. Sometimes I feel as though I should pull it all back. Most of the time, I just want to let it go. Drift. White to black. Black to white. There is a sort of existential atrophy when you decide that letting go is alright, isn't there? No one will answer that for me. I can't decide if it is too horrible a question, or too stark a reply. Once upon a time, I felt a lyrical justification for holding everything together. Odysseus trapped between Scylla and Charybdis. I wonder why anyone ever made me read *The Odyssey*. Every journey has its monsters, I suppose.

I trundle down the stairs of my apartment out into the street, bare and cold. I leave the pillows, the photographs, the lenses, then canvases, the studio, and the paint pots to wander into something surreal. Plato's reality. Beyond cave and shadow, dragging childhood's chains behind me. I forget what he looks like. He could be anyone. He could be an imposter, someone who is taking advantage of my unfortunate story. He has no imagination either way. Daddy tells me to meet him at the coffee shop. He'll buy me bacon and eggs. I'm vegan. I'll have water.

I expect that if there is a God, he is quite different than we imagine. I expect the entity we call God is beyond language, perhaps beyond gender, certainly transcending our inadequate sense of love. I expect his purple lips to part and utter code that only those that have suffered – I mean *really* suffered – will understand. Probably some dry joke that will make us all laugh. As I hobble carefully down the sidewalk, trying with every step to pull it back, to stay connected,

(I am pieces. I am only pieces)

I am sure I hear the voice of God. I am sure there is a mumble in the noise that is meant for me.

"What?" I ask. But the voice isn't clear.

"What?" I ask again. But the voice crackles and fizzes into the background.

The restaurant smells like pancake farts and too much artificial sweetener in the coffee. There's nothing here I recognize, not even the way I feel right now.

"Jenny," I hear someone call, eager. The man is grizzled, grey, his mouth carelessly wet, his face jowly as though he has suddenly lost weight. There are only the eyes I recognize. I would call him sad, but that is not the word for the way he looks at me.

"What – " I start, but find myself unable to complete the thought. I actually don't know what it is I was going to say. My legs shutter as though I were out on the tundra caught in a ruthless wind.

"Can I have a hug?" he asks. I don't know how he isn't seeing my distress. In fact, I think he looks right through me and sees something he wants to see rather than the pastiche standing in my place.

"No," I whisper, but he embraces me just the same. His breath smells astringent; his body smells of sleep and sour beer.

"I never went fishing," he tells me, though I haven't asked. "I needed to get away."

"What – "

"For a while, not far. But then I had to get lost because otherwise I would have been found."

I still don't have words. I don't have anything for him. I feel my jaw chattering as though I might have an idea to share but if this is true all thought is trapped, mute. He isn't right, I know, but I can't bring myself to tell him he is wrong.

He laughs and I don't know what's funny. He laughs like he used to when I made faces at the dinner table. He would stick a spoon to his nose or balance it on his chin, and I would laugh too loudly. I worried that he would find me out, that I was only laughing because I thought he wanted me to, that he had more fun when I was laughing than if I told him the thing with the spoon was dumb, it was old. It was old after the first time.

"It wasn't a game," he says, trying to sound earnest. "I needed to find some things out about myself, Jenny. I needed to be out in the world where the world could have a chance to recognize me."

"What – " I start again, trying to interrupt his stupidity.

"It was too much responsibility. I needed to figure out what I had to show the world."

"Did you?" I manage to stammer.

"Not yet. But I missed you, so I thought I'd try to find you." He watches for me to react, but I am still shivering, though I'm fairly certain it isn't actually all that chilly. "I honestly thought I'd never find you, that you'd be married, maybe with kids of your own. It was a surprise when you turned up so nearby."

"I want to travel," I tell him, though I don't know why this is what I say.

"Where would you go?"

It is now that the shuddering in my legs becomes a full-blown panicked seizure. We haven't ordered. We haven't even sat down. We are just standing here. Why are we just standing here, everybody watching? There is an obese man feeding French fries to a baby squeezed into a high chair. Another child at the same table is spilling salt all over her place-mat. There are a few nubs of crayons in front of her and she should be drawing, she should be drawing unicorns or fairies, rainbows, anything. Instead she is spilling salt and it is running out. My arms are shaking uncontrollably. I can hear my mouth, my tight little mouth stuttering, trying to tell him to stop, trying to tell him to be dead, to let me be, to catch me before I fall.

The walls all around me are white, the curtains at the window are drawn halfway. The section of sky that I can see is as white as the walls. I'm in the hospital or dead. Daddy is in the room. I smell him before I see him, his face pale as the sky. Like the salt, I feel myself spilling out. I don't know why I am even conscious. I sleep again until the walls are blue. He isn't here this time, but he's left his eyeglasses, so he may not have gone far. There are flowers on the sill, yellow ones. I don't know who knows I'm here or who would send flowers. I don't know how long I've been here, so perhaps the word is out there. I've finally succumbed. The blue in the sky is shifting dark. There isn't a light on in the room and I am glad at that. I want the room faded to black. One machine is humming, another drips and whirrs. I try to wish the curtains shut tight. I try to wish things the way they ought to be. Absolutely this. Or absolutely that.

A nurse brings me food covered in small, white, plastic domes. Steam erupts slowly from the largest dome in the middle of the tray. There is a cup on the tray with a lid and a straw. "Water," she says. "In case you're thirsty." She smiles. "I can put ice in it if you'd like." I feel like I should answer, but I can't bring myself to open my mouth. I just look past her. I listen to her rattle around the room. She is waiting for me to speak, follow her with my eyes, finally emit something more than air. Earlier, a doctor arrived, read the chart and then described me as having nothing wrong. An uncertain illness. Psychosomatic paralysis. I tried writing a protest but only managed a jangled scrawl. My voice fills the room in stilted illegible stutters. I use my eyes to signal, which forces everyone to guess what the next question should be. The cramps are immense, muscles pull back taught against the bone. Fleshy machines moving uncertain armatures. When the room is empty, I manage to stand. When anyone risks entering, I am resigned to the bed, sour smelling, the air around me sick with its own atmosphere.

When he sneaks back in with a couple of coffees from a machine down the hall, I am standing by the window. I think of all the lessons I have learned. I think of being undone and undone and undone. I think I have become no one. I will take him back, this riddled man, the also-ran. Give me gas. Give me a gun. Hushaby, hushaby, lay me to sleep. He is more sad than determined, more unfortunate than fool. I sit by the window, tired after sleeping, and I watch the children from the cancer ward down in the hospital rotunda with pathological curiosity. They play Ring-Around-the-Rosy. Though the glass is thick, I imagine their voices rising, "ashes, ashes, we all fall down." I feel myself welling with tears, but those are the fruit of weakness, so I choke them back. Daddy hands me a paper cup full with bitter coffee and I sip it slowly though my teeth, savouring it like wine.

While researching to find a publisher for a different piece, I read one publication's guidelines which included, "no Daddy-issue stories." The stipulation made me laugh. Then, this story spilled out like salt. Of course, I sent it to the same publisher who naturally rejected the story.

I've tried other titles, but, awkward as it is, this is the one that sticks. At one time, I used "The law of absolutes," but that was too pretentious. I imagine Jennifer as awkward, unconfident, worried. Like someone guarding a cucumber field in ancient Jerusalem. The reference to cucumber watchers is Biblical. Look it up.

Dialogue tells a character better than passages of descriptive prose. For Jennifer, her ability to express herself is choked by the men in her life. I couldn't find dialogue for her. She restrained me with her mutism. This is what I imagine, anyway. She thinks and creates in symbols. Even then, everything is borrowed. As with the character in /a simple function/, this character struggles with putting things together in her head so that they make sense. Every writer writes himself or herself. I don't care what other authors say, every character is a piece of the writer. I sometimes have feminized my fears, confusions, and anxieties in fiction. It might be easy to suggest that I write weak and inadequate female characters, so, I naturally must have critical attitudes toward women. In fact, I don't write robust, whole male characters. All my characters are equally flawed.

We all struggle to understand who our parents are. Somehow, even when they are candid with us, there's still a dark glass through which we never quite see the whole of them. If you've never read Margaret Atwood's Cat's Eye, you should. Thanks KW for suggesting Atwood's masterpiece to me long ago.

A quarter mile upstream from the Unity Street Bridge, the back lot of Andy Steinhouse's Gas n' Go overlooks the Sandalwood River. When Max Steinhouse retired eight years ago, a good piece of the town turned out to watch as Andy, adamantly coached by his father, painted out Max's name and stenciled in his own along the false front above the garage bay doors. Andy's wife, Marnie, was there too, smiling with their son, Vincent Junior (named after *her* father). At the time, she might have been pregnant. Andy couldn't remember for sure.

He stands in the doorway of his service station and looks out at an uneventful Sunday morning. The day expects to remain quiet this way until noon. That's when the church bells ring and the many loyal parishioners fill the street with their traffic. This is the pattern and cadence of the town: sober, humble, devout.

The morning's tranquility is suddenly interrupted by a bright blue convertible. Andy puzzles as the car crosses into the lot and up to the pumps. He listens to the familiar chimes as the vehicle's front and then rear tires roll across the alarm.

Like Max before him, Andy runs a full-serve business complete with window washing and optional fluid check. For Andy, it's always a quick tell that a stranger is from out-of-town when they pop right out of their car like this fellow in the aviator sunglasses, bright red forehead and thinning brown hair.

"Full up?" Andy asks.

"Sure," the driver says awkwardly, surprised at the service.

"You're not from here," Andy says.

"Nope," the fellow says. "Hey, maybe you can help me. I'm looking for someone I used to know."

The holiday and fishing crowd ask for directions, ask how to get to the hospital (the biggest one in the region), or one of the many bed-and-breakfasts in town and in the village beyond. Visitors never ask *for* someone. The town is small, but not that small.

"I grew up here," Andy says. "But I'd never claim to know everyone."

"I'm looking for this good-looking kid I knew in high school. He was an amazing football player in his day, a quarterback. They say that no one played quite as well as he did."

Andy lifts the nozzle, unscrews the convertible's gas cap, and starts pumping. These things he does automatically while he studies the driver, the way he moves his hands, nervous, determined, touching the car, the chrome on the pump, the exposed handle of the squeegee soaking in greying washer fluid. The driver is tall, heavy, his belt cinched to maintain a waistline that long ago acquiesced to the generous muffin of a gut. The man's face doesn't match anyone in memory. Age, weight, or time has filled recognition with blank spaces.

"Not me," Andy says. "I was a wide receiver."

The man suddenly smiles and slaps Andy's shoulder as though finishing a good joke. "You don't recognize me, do you?" He licks an already wet lip and nods. "I'm better looking, right? That's it, isn't it? Maybe the new haircut."

Suddenly, Andy is with him, full of tenuous recognition. *"Dave Marsden?* Wow." Andy pauses, his head rushing with snappy remarks. "I thought you said *amazing* quarterback. You didn't immediately come to mind." He smiles. "You'll have to excuse my old brain." In truth, the teenager who crawls up through Andy's memories barely matches the strange, *alternate universe* version of the Dave Marsden leaning on the hood of the car. He is at least a hundred pounds heavier, a little taller maybe, and the wardrobe is a ridiculous mix of 5th Avenue and flea market all in the same outfit. Not at all the fit, polished, preppy kid Andy knew in high school.

"Still stuck at the old Gas 'n Go, eh, Andy? I thought you might be."

The comment triggers a defensive pang. The old quarterback's arrogance has apparently not faded. "Dad retired and I took over."

"What I mean is, look at you pumping gas for me. Just like the old days. It's true that nothing ever changes around here."

Andy is quiet for a moment. They'd played on the same team, but had always been more opponents than friends. "What brings you to town?" Andy hopes to keep the attention off of their relationship or anything personal. Dave is not a *someone* he'd hoped to ever see again. In fact, since high school, he really hadn't ever found himself caught in a moment of syrupy nostalgia. Day-to-day is always better than yesterday.

Dave rounds the front of the car, his arms folded across his belly, as though forcing his hands to still. "Dad's sick. My sister called and asked me to come home. Doctor thinks he won't last another week."

"That's too bad," Andy says, genuinely sympathetic. "He's not that old, is he?"

"Sixty-three. Got cancer. Probably all the years he smoked."

"This isn't your first time back in fifteen years, is it?"

"Not really." It sounds immediately like a lie. "I think maybe a few times a long time ago, but mostly I've stayed in Manhattan. It's an amazing place, Andy-boy. You're missing out, stuck here like this."

"Who's been taking care of your dad?"

"Mom. But she gets tired. My sister is just over in Parson's Ridge, so she comes into town at least once a week. Maybe you've run into her at the grocery store."

"Nope. Haven't seen her." Andy wonders how someone could stay away from home for that long. Maybe they'd been to visit him in the city. Andy guesses that aging parents and asshole son probably do better by phone or email than face-to-face.

"So, the station's yours?" Dave points to the painted name above the door.

"Yep." Andy finishes and seats the nozzle back in its cradle.

"Look at you," Dave says. "All grown up and running the family business."

"Ya, well, it's work, right? Everybody's got to do it."

"You're right about that one, Andy-boy. Everybody toils in this world. Some more than others." Dave reaches down into the well behind the passenger's seat and produced a can of beer. "You want one?"

"Not on the job, thanks." Andy watches the driver crack the can and punch back at least half of it in one draw. There are only a few cans left stranded in the plastic yoke. Another twisted plastic yoke lies behind the driver's seat. "Should you be driving?"

Dave ignores him. "The place could use a coat of paint, eh, Andy-boy? That would freshen it up a bit."

"Dad and I are going to do that this summer." Andy wonders why he suddenly feels so defensive. "No one complains. The coffee is the best in town."

"Really?"

"That's what they say."

"And I guess the fact that you still offer full-service brings people around."

"I think we do better than the Shell station over on Palmerston."

"Good for you, buddy," Dave wanders toward the entrance of the garage. "Good for you, Andy-boy. Good for you."

Andy watches Dave disappear into the mouth of the service bay. The area is empty. Just the same, if his dad was here, he would have heard him yelling at Dave to get out. "Hey, Dave," Andy calls. "What have you been up to?"

"Just looking at your tools."

"In Manhattan, I mean?" Andy drags the squeegee across the front windshield of the convertible, scrapping a crop of mayflies as it goes.

Dave pokes his head out and waves a socket wrench in a pink fist. "It's pretty cool in here. Your hands must get pretty dirty."

"Some days."

"I'm divorced," Dave says, weaving two conversations together. "Three years now. No kids."

"Sorry to hear that."

"I get laid whenever I want though. It's better than marriage. Cheaper too."

Andy is about to make some reference to dirty hands, but stops himself. "How's your job?"

"Since Oh-Eight, not so good. I'm keeping it above water though. That's better than most."

"Good to hear," Andy says, and strolls toward the station. "I like your car."

"Rental," Dave says. "What do I owe you?"

"Twenty-five by the pump, but I'll knock ten off for you."

"You don't have to."

"Call it the *old friend* discount," Andy says. "Come on inside, I'll ring it up."

"I thought the *old friend* discount might be a free tank, but I'll take what I can get." He slaps Andy on the shoulder again, more drunken-aggressive than friendly.

Andy ignores him. He should charge him more for being a prick. The inside of the station is probably no match to the high-rise office he imagines Dave occupies every day. The Formica counter is stained with grease and cluttered with lottery tickets, invoices, mints, and the transaction machine that connects Dave's small business to the bank. Out on the floor, there is a rack of candy bars, another with canned beans, Hamburger Helper, macaroni and cheese, and another with toiletries for the tourists. Nothing fancy. Behind the counter, there is a wire rack with a collection of local maps. Most travellers already have a GPS unit in their car. Andy has considered replacing the maps with romance novels or crossword puzzle magazines, but even those are becoming old fashioned. There is a wooden case back there too where his dad used to house a display of plastic car models they built together when Andy was young enough to enjoy that sort of thing. Andy emptied it a year or two ago but never found anything else to decorate it with. There is one item left from Dad's collection. On the top shelf, displayed in a wooden saddle his dad built: A worn, dusty football.

"Is that what I think it is?" Dave asks right away.

"Game ball."

"How'd you get that? I thought it went to the school?"

"It did," Andy tells him. "It was in the trophy case for a long time. They renovated ten or so years ago when Coach Nelson retired. Coach asked dad if he wanted the ball. They were friends, remember?"

"Should be mine, shouldn't it? I threw the thing."

"I caught it," Andy says softly, annoyed by his Sunday morning customer. "Cash or charge?"

Andy expects a gold Amex card, but instead, Dave rifles through a wrinkled roll of bills and drops a couple of twenties on the smudged countertop. Andy punches the total into the till and hands his adversary his change.

"You have to admit, that was the best pass this town has ever seen."

"It was a pretty good catch, too." Andy hands Dave his receipt.

"But without the pass you'd have nothing to catch."

"Sure, but without the catch, it just would have been a Hail Mary."

"It was nothing like that. I aimed it right to you. A perfect spiral."

"Wow," Andy laughs, but stops himself before mocking. "History likes to do her nails up pretty, doesn't she?"

"What's that supposed to mean?"

"That ball was going nowhere. You just didn't want to be holding it when the clock ran down."

"You think you deserve to have the game ball?" Dave's voice is loud in the small shop, the man's hands flicker open and shut spastically.

"Yes, I do," Andy says proudly.

"You know it's the quarterback that matters, right? There are plenty of receivers. There's only one of me. You're lucky I picked you to receive for me. I think that pass still holds the record for longest winning pass in the district. Isn't that true?"

"I don't know about that, Dave. I know ten guys who could have thrown a wild ball like that. I don't know too many guys who could have caught it. What did they used to call a throw like that?"

"I don't know what you're talking about. I through a perfect spiral."

"A duck. That's what they used to call a throw like that one, Dave. Wobble, wobble, wobble, like flight came upon it as some sort of miracle." Andy could tell by Dave's face that he had said too much. Dave had hooked him and Andy had taken the bait. In this moment, he regretted not redirecting this menace up to the Shell the moment his tires hit the pavement. *Out of gas,* he should have said.

Dave rocks back and forth as though he might leap over the counter and grab the ball. "You think *you* could throw that far?"

"I'm not doing this with you, Dave. I'm not having a cock fight on a Sunday morning. I haven't even finished my first coffee."

"You're a has-been, right? You, and this station, and this whole town."

"What are you doing, Dave?"

"Show me you can throw the ball."

"You couldn't throw it any farther or any better than you could in high school. Look at you. You're a mess. You shouldn't even be driving." Andy feels the deep disappointment of arriving beyond restraint. "I could give that thing distance, Dave. I'm not saying anyone could catch it, but I could throw it."

"Now, or *once upon a time?*"

"Now." Something sinks in him and he knows he's committed to something that can only end badly.

"Come on, then," Dave taunts. "You've got a ball. Let's go out there and make a couple of friendly passes. I'm sure we could measure ninety yards out to the sidewalk."

"You didn't throw ninety yards," Andy says roughly. "You threw eighty and I ran in the last ten."

"It was eighty from the scrimmage, and I backed up at least ten, maybe fifteen."

"Whatever," Andy says.

"We'll mark eighty and see how you do."

"I told you, I'm not doing this."

Dave pulls the wad of bills and drops it on the counter. "My life's savings."

Andy hits a button on the register and the cash drawer rolls open with a ding. "Well, you're out of luck. I don't think I have more than the forty you gave me in here. Everyone pays with cards nowadays." Andy has yesterday's deposit tucked under the cash drawer, but he isn't about to pull that money out. He's got bills to pay. Marnie would never forgive him for betting like this.

"My life savings for yours, Andy-boy. Come on, Stinkhouse, don't be a wimp."

Anytime he fumbled, the locker room crowd had another name for Andy Steinhouse. He never got used to the insult. Instead, he played impeccably so that the name became a shame for most players to utter. Anyway, being called *Stinkhouse* by a few teammates was nowhere as devastating as a crowd of spectators erupting into honks and quacks. Andy smiles at Dave and knows the old quarterback is playing dirty on purpose. "Why'd you come here, Dave?"

"I told you. To see my parents."

"I mean, here. To the station. You could have driven in and out of town without hassling me. Did you come to see me because you have something to prove?"

"I stopped for gas and to say *hey*," Dave says, pouting falsely. "That's all. You're the one who is making a big deal out of this football thing."

Andy slips forty cash from the till and sets it on the counter next to the dirty wad of bills. Dave smiles. "I'm going to win this one," Andy says. "You're already broke."

"Don't worry about it." Dave smirks. "Do you need me to reach the ball for you? It's up there a little high."

"I think I can manage." Andy lifts the prize ball from its wooden cradle.

"Have you got an old tire or something to mark the distance?"

"Grab that hubcap holding the door open." Andy walks into the garage and takes a moment to pump some air into the soft pigskin.

The pair mosey out to the end of the island by the gas pumps. "Eighty yards," he says to his teammate.

"Eighty," Dave says and starts pacing. They quickly run out of blacktop and have to pace along the sidewalk.

"We're not likely to see much traffic this time of day," Andy warns. "Let's just keep to one side of the road, though, just in case." He follows reluctantly, measuring the distance himself. He isn't worried about throwing or catching. The whole contest just seems a waste of time. What he feels is a little tired, like he's being pulled to a place he won't easily escape.

Dave drops the tarnished chrome hubcap down in the dirt by the roadside. "Alright, let's go back and I'll throw first."

Andy follows him back quietly and watches Dave juggle the ball up into the air, trying to get it to spin just right. He has a feeling that Dave hadn't really thrown a ball in a very long time. He is huffing like a dog that has been run to exhaustion. Large stains blossom under Dave's armpits and across his chest. His hair is matted with sweat. Near to where today's encounter began, Dave runs his scuffed loafer in a line to mark scrimmage. He punches Andy in the shoulder, urging him. "Ready," he calls, as though they are out on the grass with a capacity crowd hollering support.

"You want me to *run* out there?"

"Of course, Stinkhouse. Did you think I was going to drive you?" Dave is already pumping his arm against an imaginary clock. "Go!"

Andy canters to the edge of the gas station while Dave taunts him.

"Come on *Stink*, get a move on."

"Whatever," Andy says to himself. He watches the hubcap getting closer. Sixty yards out he twists his body with a rhythm and grace that is in him like an instinct. Dave launches the pass. As the ball arcs high overhead it begins to wobble, side to side at first, but then it rolls over once, then twice. The ball catches in its own chaos and begins plummeting. The duck bounces against the pavement short of where Andy skids to change directions. He scrambles down into the ditch and manages to get one hand on it and pull the ball in before it bounces a second time. He looks down at his feet, glad he is wearing work shoes. They are greased in mud and slime.

"You missed, Stinkhouse!" Dave shouts as Andy hikes back to the station.

"That was a mess. How was I supposed to catch that?" Andy hears an embarrassing swath of competitive teenager in his own voice.

"Give me a do-over," Dave says.

"Not a chance," Andy says. "We do this once. Your turn to run."

Andy lobs the ball in the air, just to get a feel for it. He stretches his arm in a wide circle.

"Out of shape, Stink?"

"Just run," Andy says. Dave snaps off the line and ambles across the grey asphalt. Andy waits, counts, and then launches the ball high and clear. Dave turns late and the spiral hits him hard in the shoulder and bounces away. Andy laughs but stops quickly. He watches Dave dance around the ball bobbing up and down on the road. Luck would send a car flying around the bend to knock the king of ducks out of the game. Instead, the town is cloistered in church or asleep. The birds twitter and the crickets chirp. Dave finishes dancing and sweats his way back to Andy's Gas n' Go.

"You timed it wrong," Dave calls to him. He repeats the charge as he chuffs back to the line. "You timed it wrong. I wasn't ready."

"You didn't catch it."

"You didn't catch mine, it bounced."

"You didn't even get it to me," Andy says. "I was ready for it."

"At least I was on my mark," Dave says.

Andy tries to calm the conversation. "You want a drink? Something softer than beer?"

"What about the do-over?"

"Maybe later," Andy says. "Drink?"

"How about a beer?"

"I've got cold lemonade."

"Lemonade would be great."

"I think I can spot you one." Andy isn't sure how he landed in the ridiculous contest in the first place. Certainly, there wasn't a winner. Just as surely, Andy knew, Dave would dress it up as though Andy lost. "Let's go inside. You keep your money. I'll keep mine." Dave is still holding on to the ball and Andy has a strange feeling that it might not make it back up to the shelf.

"You married?" Dave asks.

"Yep," Andy says, still a little winded from the run.

"So, who'd you end up with?"

"What do you mean?"

"Who'd you marry?"

When Dave Marsden finished high school, he hung around for the summer and worked at his uncle's lumber yard, but before August was up, he left for college without fanfare. For the three previous years, Dave and Marnie Wilde had been a rock-steady couple in the high school halls. Captain of the football team, head cheerleader, king and queen of the prom. They even sat on student council together. When he skipped town, Dave didn't give her the courtesy of goodbye. Instead, he left a note with her mom. "Thanks for everything," it read.

Andy feels suddenly weak, groggy, and even a little dizzy. Football, after all, is just a game. Women are something different. "I've been married to Marnie for twelve years," he says quietly.

Dave doesn't seem to be paying attention and Andy hopes he might shift the conversation to something safer. "You mean that girl from over in Camden with the weird front tooth?"

"No, Dave. Marnie Wilde."

The man whose best throw in fifteen years turned out to be a lame duck stops dead on the pavement outside of Andy's Gas 'n Go. His shoes even make a scuffing sound in the dirt like a couple of skidding bicycle tires. It was a mistake, Andy thinks, to have told him. Dave flashes a sudden look that Andy can only compare to the many faces of mass murderers that he had seen in the news. The sad hulk's hands are still, resting at the man's sides. Another flash and Dave is grinning, moving again. He holds the door for Andy.

"I forgot something in the car," Dave says, tosses Andy the ball, and actually jogs over to the rented convertible. Andy thinks he might be watching the man bolt. He'd paid for the gas, so no big deal, but the rest of it, the sudden bounce in his step, the strange darkness in the man's eye; he shivers, unsure why he feels so uneasy, so nervous inside. His own hands might feel a little shaky and unsteady.

Except for their connection with Dave, Andy's courtship with Marnie hadn't been unusual. She was supposed to go away to college, but worked on correspondence courses instead. She finished a degree at the community college, got a job as a nurse over at the Peter J. Wainwright Medical Center, and they were perfectly happy together raising the two boys and a dog named Beau. Even early on, there had been very little talk of Dave between him. He was barely even a ghost in the town. It suddenly occurs to Andy that Dave isn't in town to make small talk with his former teammate. Dave came back to claim a trophy he'd jilted long ago.

Andy watches him through the dusty window. Dave reached into the car, stuffs something in the pocket of his khaki pants then smiles contentedly as he strolls back across the lot, chest puffed as far as it will go, but not beyond the man's belly. He lifts his head and squints at the bright sun, stops, shakes his arms and hands as he did after a huddle, readying himself for the next play. Andy rests the ball next to the register. He walks to the large cooler and grabs a couple of lemonade-flavoured sodas. He isn't particularly thirsty or worn from the ball toss, but he suspects that Dave might be a heartbeat away from a coronary. Andy wonders if he really bedded as many women as his comments suggested. Mid-thirties, balding, overweight, and more than just a little arrogant: not a recipe Andy associated with a good catch, but then again, people in the city might all be as desperate as Dave seems.

"Here you are." Andy hands him a bottle.

"It sure is warm out there today." Dave walks over and leans against the counter. Andy stands in the middle of the shop, bread and few canned goods to his left, candy bars and gum to his right. It isn't much of an empire, but he feels that he must be inordinately happier than this unexpected rival.

"Why'd you come here, Dave?" The question is repetitive, but Andy hadn't really heard the truth yet.

"I told you, to see about my dad."

"I mean, why stop here to see me?"

"Old friends." Dave says, taking a gulp of pink.

"We weren't ever that, right? You know we were always at each other."

"Easy, Andy." Dave says, his false smile fades. "I needed gas. I wanted to, you know, check in on you."

"You said you were divorced. You came looking for Marnie, didn't you?"

"She still look good in blue jeans?"

"I knew it."

"Calm yourself, brother. I'm not interested in some wide-hipped country girl."

"You wanted to rub it in my face that you're big city and I'm the little country mouse, is that it?"

Dave sucks on the bottle again and nearly empties it. A fresh wash of sweat drips down his forehead. "Aren't we the same, you and me, two old teammates, once celebrated, now fighting to make our way in the world?"

"That's the difference, Dave. I'm not fighting. I wasn't fighting in high school. I wasn't fighting on the field. It's never been a fight for me."

"I still hear it. Don't you?"

"What's that?"

"You know? The roar of the crowd." Dave turns his back to look out the dusty window. "Don't you chase the victory, Stinkhouse? Don't you wish for that feeling all of the time?"

"That's really pathetic, Dave," Andy says. "I'm sorry you feel you have something to prove. I don't want to fight with you. I don't have anything to prove to you. I'm happy with my life. I wouldn't want yours. I didn't at seventeen, and I don't want your life now."

Dave smiles that ominous grin again. "I'm sorry I make you nervous."

"You don't make me nervous," Andy says quickly, but it isn't true. He is annoyed that it shows enough for Dave to catch him in the lie.

"I bet your father keeps a 12-gauge under the counter for protection. You ever been robbed?"

To Andy, it is the strangest question in the world. "No gun," he lies again, "But there are a couple of cameras in the shop and over the pumps. Every time the prices go up, someone feels the need to run before paying."

"No gun?"

"Roy Stephens still has his gun shop down the road if you're looking," Andy says. He studies Dave now, worried about his interest in the security of his little gas station. Dave appears sane enough, but who could say. He isn't sure what six or eight beers, divorce, and economic collapse might do to a former football hero who could no longer throw a ball. These days, there seems to be a thread of chaos in everything that never wants to settle. The money was still on the counter.

"Here, Dave. Take your money. Take mine too. Let's call it a tie, but you won."

"She's good in the sack, isn't she? Does she still purr like a cat when you lick her ear?"

"Marnie never slept with you, Dave. She told me that."

"You believed her?" The monster laughs. His hands are back to touching things, smoothing the papers on the counter, straightening the transaction machine. There are more than a few flies bouncing against the window, trapped in the heat drawing them there.

Andy moves back behind the counter and wipes around the money with a rag he keeps in his pocket. The cleaning doesn't make a difference to the stains. It is time to close this transaction and send Dave on his way. He holds out the money. "Are we done here?"

"I'm just shooting the breeze, old buddy. I missed you." Dave grabs a candy bar from the rack, tears it open, and takes a bite. "Don't you want to catch up?"

"I've got work to do. Take the money."

Andy was held up once, back in his teens. He knew enough to open the cash register rather than reach for the .22 pistol under the counter. When his dad retired, Andy cleared it out of the shop. The gun gave Marnie the willies. When a gas-bar attendant down in Hopewell Springs was shot to death three years ago, she changed her mind and bought him a big Smith & Wesson for the shop. "Like the one in the movies," she said. "I want you to scare them with the gun so you don't have to shoot anyone."

Dave wanders around the little shop, slowly at first, like he can't find the exit. He touches the inventory as though blessing it. Andy thinks about what a hustle life in the city must be. The term *rat race* makes a strange kind of sense as he watches Dave sweep around blindly.

"You got a dog or something?" Andy asks, trying to find something pleasant to chat about. He is used to having short conversations about nothing. That is the extent of his manner with customers. *The weather is fair, the economy less so. Your engine has a tick. You should bring it in for me to have a look.* He doesn't argue with people. He certainly never gets down to reminiscing with anyone about the day he caught the ball that won the state championship for the first time since before the Korean War. Nobody has won it since, but there seems to be enough noise out there that people in town had forgotten, or let it fade as it should.

Dave is holding a gun. It looked like a 9mm. He isn't waving the weapon around, isn't making a point of having it. It is just dangling there at the end of the man's soft arm. The thing is silver, but dull. Andy thinks of Marnie and the boys. He reaches under the counter without taking his eyes off of Dave. He touches the magnum and a jolt of adrenaline shoots through him, uncomfortable, startling. What he needs is a panic button, but there is a monthly fee for that particular security device.

"You okay, Dave?"

"Just fine," the man says, but continues wandering. He looks up at the clock above the door. "I guess I'm about out of time," he says. A moment later, he blurts: "I have an idea."

Anything, Andy thinks, *to get him out of here and on his way.* "What is it?"

"Give me a do-over and you can keep the cash."

"I don't want the money."

"Do-over," Dave says, his eyes cold now, the smile gone.

"Sure," Andy says, nervous. "Am I catching or throwing?"

"I'll catch first," Dave says. In a swift, remarkable motion, Dave snaps the ball from the counter with his free hand, though still not trying to hide the weapon.

"Go ahead," Andy says, and points down behind the counter. "My boot is untied." As he crouches, he grabs the heavy handgun and shoves it in the deep pocket of his work pants.

"I'll wait."

He unties and ties his muddy shoe and worries that Dave saw his hand move under the counter. When he stands again, Dave smiles, the strangest look Andy has ever seen.

"Go ahead out," Andy says. As he moves to the exit, Dave stalls in the doorway, the small pistol raised toward him. Tensely, Andy pulls the magnum, which catches in his pocket and tears the fabric. Oddly, Dave just stands there, facing him, watching, smiling. No matter how many times Andy had fired the thing at Roy Stephens's pistol range (which wasn't often) there was no preparing for pulling a gun on another human being. He points it, tries to hold the barrel still. The moment feels suddenly draped in scales, the light works differently, too dim and too bright at the same time.

"A duel," Dave smirks. He considers both raised weapons carefully. He laughs. "I bet I'm a better shot. No duck this time, Andy-boy."

"We're not playing, Dave. You need to go."

"Eighty yards or ninety?"

"Drop the gun, Dave. I don't know what you're up to, but I don't want anyone to get hurt. We're two old friends, right? Isn't that what you said earlier? I don't believe you're well…"

Dave moves quickly for a man as large and worn out as he looks. He drops the thing he'd been holding and it makes a hollow, plastic sound as it hits the old linoleum floor. Dave kicks it and it skitters away. Andy glances to watch the toy slide under one of the grocery racks. In the same beat, Dave clasps both hands over the Smith & Wesson, one mitt clamps Andy's hand against the grip and the other over the trigger guard.

Andy can't move his hands without losing control of the weapon. He remembers a story his mother read to him once, a long lifetime ago, about a monkey trap. A small hole in an old stump and a banana is all you needed to catch a monkey. Andy doesn't feel as simian as he does completely Neanderthal. He is caught in a survival moment; his only instinct is to freeze.

"Do you ever feel like your best days are behind you?"

"No," Andy says. "Never."

"You don't look back there and think, that was my moment, that was it and now everything else is a footnote?" Dave's eyes have sunken too deeply into his skull, two black dead things that don't look like they're focussing properly.

"No," Andy repeats, struggling against Dave's vise-like hold on the gun. The man's hands are sweaty, twitchy, but iron tight on him.

"I'm surprised that your daddy didn't frame the picture from the paper."

"What?" Andy stutters the word.

"After the game, there was an article in the paper. The reporter described our relationship. Don't you remember that?"

"No."

"They called us Cain and Abel. It has a better ring than Jacob and Esau I suppose." Dave smiles, that same eerie, contrived smile. "You made the cover of the newspaper, big and colourful. You don't remember?"

"No," Andy says again, certain that the story isn't true.

"The photographer must have been waiting for you in the end zone. You filled the foreground while I was just a dithered collection of grey and white dots in the background."

Andy feels Dave's finger fishing around the trigger guard. "This time, I'll catch the front page, old buddy, and you, you'll be a smear at the bottom of page two. This is your moment." Dave grins and winks. "I always thought that this would be an exhilarating way to…" The big gun Marnie bought him to scare hoodlums away explodes and Dave's head disappears, his body drops. Andy's first thought is *I'm going to hell.*

The first bell makes Andy nearly jump out of his skin. The second bell reminds him that it is Sunday in the quiet town and church all over town is about to end. The bells on all of Stockton Commons' eight churches clang the noon hour. The third bell reminds him of the long tradition that has existed in this part of town since before Andy could remember. A group of dad's old friends walk the six blocks from St. Sebastian's Anglican Church and spread a good word and share a coffee with his dad, one of the town's few atheists. The group had grown to include wives, children, and lately, grandchildren. Andy has about fifteen minutes before the group will cross into the shop despite the fact that his retired father, Max, hadn't joined the gang for coffee in more than a year. Andy remembers that he forgot to put the second coffee pot on to brew.

But there are darker, more urgent matters just now. He has twelve minutes before they will be within eyesight of the car still sitting by the pumps. He considers driving it into the garage bay. There is another tradition that has existed nearly as long as the St. Sebastian's gang has been visiting. Max Steinhouse would leave the garage doors open wide to make sure everyone in town knew that there was no one in there secretly breaking the Sabbath any more than necessary. The pumps remained open. Fuel, after all, was as essential as the police force or the fire department. Wayne Gilmorgan had made a promise to Max that if any stranger came through town on a Sunday and needed car repairs, well, they were welcome for a free night's stay at Gilmorgan's Bed & Breakfast if they'd wait until Monday to have their car repaired. No stranger had ever come through town for repairs, and certainly no one had ever been rewarded with a free night at the Gilmorgan's house. Andy didn't know if that was a genuine miracle or just some statistically insignificant fact.

There is a car on the tarmac and nowhere to hide it.

Most of the time, the river behind the station is a muddy slough. After a hard rain, it can run as dangerously high and wild as the Missouri. The gas station had only flooded once and the damage hadn't been all that bad. The banks of the river through town were reinforced with caged stone. Near the bridge, however, the banks were left natural because the bedrock was exposed and the shoreline was thus protected against erosion. As a kid, Andy sometimes walked down the bank to jump off the low part of the bridge into the murky water.

Besides throwing it up on the hoist and hoping the Sunday crowd wouldn't ask about it, pushing the shiny, sporty convertible into the depths of the Sandalwood River seemed to be the only other option. It is a terrible idea, and Andy knows it. The car might bog down in the mud, half in and half out. Long contemplative moments pass, and Andy is stuck in the doorway. Only a few birds are singing in the trees across the street. The crickets have gone quiet. The bells stop, ten-eleven-twelve, ringing.

The day is crisp, the sun not quite piercing the clouds. There are moments which shape our lives and Andy Steinhouse is stalled in the doorway of his shop trying to will time's arrow in a different direction. He watches a pair of squirrel's scolding each other as they race along the electrical wires running above the sidewalk where he recently outplayed his old rival. Presently, that same rival found a way to damn him with a vengeance and insanity that Andy cannot wrap his head around. It is already five past twelve.

"This is your moment, Andy-boy," he whispers coldly to himself.

Andy steps toward the car and suddenly remembers that there is a body on the ground in front of him and that he is still holding the murder weapon in his hand. He wonders how he could have misplaced such a thing in his short-term memory. Blood oozes freely from the head wound. Andy thinks the pool is deep and wide enough to skip rocks across. There is a long hose just inside the garage. Even if it were as powerful as a fire hose, Andy estimates it would take forever to clean this mess. There isn't enough bleach in the county to wash away this stain. He has some cleaning to do. For now, the body will have to go where the car is going.

He feels himself dragging an old tire rim from the garage, watches himself strap it to the body with a shank of polyester rope. A tarp appears from nowhere, and the body is being rolled up inside the tarp, bound, and then dragged behind the old shop and down into the river. Andy watches his arms lift the tire rim and hurl it like a discus into the depths. The body skims the surface and then sinks in one heavy swallow. He is knee deep in the drink before he thinks about what he is doing.

A cold shock runs through his belly as he imagines a set of car keys in the pocket of the pants that are now under water three or four yards from shore. Fortunately, he finds them dangling from the ignition. Andy backs the car down toward the water to a stony place where tire tracks will be hard to detect. He releases the transmission into neutral, closed the door, and delicately pushes the vehicle into the river. The thing protests, burbles, yaws, and pitches, but it sinks without hanging up in the mud or catching on a rock. The river runs on and the evidence disappears.

He stands there, the cold river licking around his knees, his boots ruined, his pants clinging to him. *What is it that Dave said? This is my moment?* He'd spent all of his time on the football field looking backwards. That's what you did as a receiver, always looking over your shoulder. With a sudden nervous instinct, Andy Steinhouse looks behind him. A small group of gawkers are standing out on the sidewalk in their Sunday best. The children are silent. Some of the women cover their mouths. One of the men steps forward and then stops. Andy sees what they see. He is covered in blood and gore. The back end of the car really isn't buried in the river. And Dave. Dave is laughing. Is he quacking? Like a Duck? Dave has a big hole in his face, but he is frolicking in the water, his hands splashing around like the whole thing is a big joke. Quack. Quack. Quack.

There is a thread of chaos that runs through everything. In the driveway, Andy imagines (or maybe he can see) a trail of blood draining from the doorway of the old shop down to the gutter near the sidewalk and anointing some of the gawkers' shoes as it flows.

One of the older children finds the trophy football in the dust and before Andy can protest, the boy launches a perfect spiral which spins high over the mess and plunges into the Sandalwood without even a splash. Despite the perfection of the throw, the ball flies way beyond Andy's reach.

Most literary publication don't accept stories over three or four thousand words long. This story is too long and I never found a home for it.

The words I use are tremendously important. That's probably a dumb thing for a writer to say. But, some writers are storytellers and some writers are poets. I tend to the poetic use of language rather than the prosaic (think: grocery list). For this piece, from the title forward, I wanted the story to be told and didn't finagle with the words. Re-read *Swamp Thing* and think about the use of language. In my humble opinion, *Swamp* is a ridiculous story that sits back on its language for strength. *Duck* is a story without any adornment to elevate it to literature. If you've wondered why a writer like Stephen King hasn't won a Pulitzer, its that he's a storyteller first. Some critics struggle to call his work literary. Read King's *Lisey's Story*, which easily deserves a grand literary award. It's one of my top 10 best reads.

I like the title, which references a badly thrown football – called a duck – but, also, *ducking* is what we do when something is coming at us that we can't avoid. Andy should have ducked when he first saw Dave's car pulling onto the lot. But looking back is never good.

We began this journey together, twelve stories ago, in the depths of something terrible. Its fitting we end in the same place. Thank you for coming along with me. DL/Nov 2017.